F. Talbot O'Donoghue

**Donnington Hall**

A Novel

F. Talbot O'Donoghue

**Donnington Hall**
*A Novel*

ISBN/EAN: 9783337032906

Printed in Europe, USA, Canada, Australia, Japan

Cover: Foto ©Andreas Hilbeck / pixelio.de

More available books at **www.hansebooks.com**

# DONNINGTON HALL:

## A Novel.

BY THE

## REV. F. TALBOT O'DONOGHUE, B.A.,

VICAR OF TICKENHAM, SOMERSET, AND CHAPLAIN TO THE MARQUIS OF
WESTMEATH; AUTHOR OF "ST. KNIGHTON'S KEIVE," ETC.

LONDON:

SAUNDERS, OTLEY, AND CO.,

66, BROOK STREET, W.

MDCCCLXV.

LONDON:

WILLIAM STEVENS, PRINTER, 37, BELL YARD,

TEMPLE BAR.

# DONNINGTON HALL.

## CHAPTER I.

"WELL, I am glad it is all over at last!" exclaimed Sir John De Marbury, throwing himself into an easy-chair in his library at Donnington Hall, in Cheshire. "It has been nothing but a scene of eating, and drinking, and speechifying from early dawn; and then to have to hear one's own praises sung at such a prodigious rate! such prophecies too of one's well-doing! I am heartily tired, I know."

"You see, John," said a grave, middle-aged lady, who was the only other occupant of the room, "you *may* get weary of pleasure itself."

B

"But I say, mother," went on the young man, gaily, for he had no idea of being taken in for a lecture on this the very day of his coming of age, "how the little curate *did* lay it on! I thought he was coming it rather strong, with a vengeance; and so I fancy did Mr. Hulton. I don't think he very much admired Mr. Jones's display of eloquence."

"I suppose Mr. Jones has an eye upon one of your livings. He thinks you may give him one in return for all the fine things he has been saying about you."

"Catch me, indeed, doing anything of the sort! Besides, I don't like him myself. He is a great deal too 'bumptious' for me."

"By the way, John, wasn't it rather odd that Mr. Hulton should have kept away from the dinner in the way he did, only just coming in for a few moments, after the cloth was removed, to propose your health, and then going away again? I thought it odd."

"Oh, he explained all about it to me. This is some saint's day or other—St. Peter's day, I think he said—and, as he has always his two services on these days, with the Communion, and as Jones wished so much to be here, why, the rector had to stay at home for the services, and was just able to slip over for half an hour in order to say his say—to show his sympathy upon the 'joyful occasion,' as he called it. I like Hulton. He is a gentleman, and means well, I think."

"It is a pity he is so dreadfully High Church; yet he was not so when your father gave him the living. I remember when he used to dance at all the Newchurch assemblies. I see him now, turning round to the orchestra, and clapping his white-kid-gloved hands as a sign for them to change the quadrille. Ah, he has altered since those days! I only hope it is for the better."

"Well, I *do* confess myself that I have rather a dislike to seeing parsons in the ball-room or hunting-field. I think they may find quite enough to do at home in their parishes."

"Oh, of course I don't mean *that*. But, as Mr. Marshall says, all this will-worship. and saint's-day services, and chanting, is sadly in-

consistent with the simplicity of our Protestant
worship."

"Well, as you know, mother, there is no great
love lost between Mr. Hulton and Mr. Marshall.
Marshall always classes Papists and Tractarians
together, and, I believe, considers the rector every
bit as bad as Mr. Delawney, the priest."

"Was the priest at the dinner to-day? I haven't
noticed him going about."

"Oh, that he was, and as jolly as ever. He
seemed quite to enjoy the exhibition poor Jones
was making of himself after dinner. Poor little
fellow! I imagine an extra glass of wine or two
quite upsets him. But I saw that Hulton was
annoyed."

As the reader will have gathered, Sir John De
Marbury, upon this 29th day of June, 184—, attained his twenty-first year, and was put in legal
possession of the Donnington Hall estates, in
Cheshire. There had been a long minority, and,
under the judicious management of Lady De
Marbury, aided by her experienced man of
business at Newchurch, Mr. Ardern, the property

had somewhat improved in value by the time the son came of age. But still it required very careful nursing, as the late Sir Richard had got into great difficulties, owing to his passion for buying land, which, in the end, never paid, or even so much as covered the interest of the money he had been obliged to borrow for the purpose. In consequence, Sir Richard De Marbury died greatly involved, and his estates, heavily encumbered, passed, along with the title, to his only son, then a child. Though matters had improved, as we have said, during the minority, yet Sir John De Marbury was soon to learn, after all the bustle and feasting were over, that, though nominally the owner of six thousand a year, yet, after his mother's jointure and other charges upon the property were paid, he had scarcely as many hundreds to live upon. This was rather a let-down to his pride—a slight abatement to his satisfaction upon taking possession of the property. However, Mr. Ardern, in the course of a long and confidential sitting, soon after the termination of the coming-of-age festivities, explained to Sir

John that his affairs, though embarrassed at the time, were not irremediably so.

"We must sell," said the lawyer, "some of the purchased property, if nothing else can be done. But, before we do this," went on Mr. Ardern, for he saw that the young man winced at the suggestion, "we can have recourse to other measures, about which there will be no difficulty now that you are of age. We must sell the next presentations to Donnington, and also Sproston."

"Poor Jones, and his expectations!" thought Sir John to himself; but he only said, "And you think this is absolutely necessary? I don't much care about Sproston, but I should have liked to have kept Donnington in my own hands; some man might get it whom I shouldn't like."

"Well, you must take your chance of that. They are both good livings, and I think I can find you purchasers without difficulty. Indeed, I happen to know of a Manchester man——"

"Oh, dear!" exclaimed Sir John—

"——who would be glad to buy Donnington for his son, now a boy at school. He would give a

good price for it too ; and then the Rector of Sproston is an old man, and the living is sure to drop
soon. Altogether, I could ensure you several
thousand pounds in this way; and then, with
this money, we could pay off some of the mort-
gagees."

" Oh, then, you will want all the money," said
Sir John, with rather a blank expression.

" Why, of course ; by this means you will have
something more of an income to live upon. I
don't say," went on Mr. Ardern, good-humouredly,
and by way of throwing in a sop, "that we
may not spare you a few hundreds for any purpose
you have a fancy for."

" A few hundreds won't go far. But never
mind ; it can't be helped."

" And then another thing has occurred to me
within the last few days. You are paying very
high interest on the mortgages—in no case less
than six per cent., and in some cases practically
ten per cent. Now there is an old fellow in Newchurch, rich as Crœsus—I mean old Delves—of
whom you have heard, I dare say, plenty of stories.

Well, I know that he would have no objection to lend money for reasonable interest upon a safe mortgage. Indeed, he told me as much not long ago, when we were doing some little business together in my office. Now suppose we were to borrow, say, £10,000 from him at four or five per cent., and pay off some of these people; why, that would put some hundreds a year in your pocket at once."

"If you can only manage it with the old fellow, of course I shall be delighted."

"I think I can;" and with these words the lawyer bundled up his papers, swallowed a mouthful of luncheon, and was off in his gig for Newchurch.

At Sir John De Marbury's age pecuniary difficulties seldom appear very formidable; and, being a good-looking young fellow enough, with plenty of spirits, and with his title and estate (such as it was), he was not unnaturally disposed to take rather a bright view of things in general, and to rely with implicit faith upon Mr. Ardern's making everything straight for him. Sir John had a great opinion too, though he didn't show it more than he could help, of his own consequence as a baronet—the only one in that part of Cheshire; and, then, was he not a De Marbury, the representative of one of the oldest families in the county, whose ancestor, Robertus Latronus, had come over with the Conqueror? and were not those his ancestors—De Marburys—those cross-legged knights who were to be seen at Donnington Church? It must be admitted that Sir John sometimes talked rather big about his " ancestors," and made a few mistakes when he got upon the subject. He was not wanting in intelligence, though not what would be called clever, but was awfully vain. For, between you and myself, reader, there was not a drop of the De Marbury blood after all in Sir John's veins, and Robertus Latronus, and those knights-templar in the chancel of Donnington Church, were no more his ancestors than they were yours or mine. The truth of the matter is, that Sir John De Marbury's grandfather, old Dr. Hibbert, being the Rector of Donnington, had married a half-sister (by the same mother, but not by the same father) of the last of the old line, Sir Hugh De Marbury, who, dying without issue, and without any other near relations of his own, left all his property to his half-sister's son, Richard Hibbert, who was very shortly afterwards transmuted, by Royal permission under the sign manual, into Richard De Marbury; and, upon his marrying a daughter of Lord Clapham, the possessor of large estates in Lancashire, and a man of great political influence at the time, the De Marbury baronetcy was revived in the person of the actual possessor of Donnington, and from him, as already narrated, both title and estates passed to the son. So that, altogether, when Sir John De Marbury produced his splendidly emblazoned genealogical tree, or dwelt upon the gallant deeds of sundry of the De Marburys (which he had read of in Dr. Flummery's County History), and when he talked with contempt of such and such a one being a *novus homo*, though undoubtedly an impression *was* produced upon young Mr. Jones, the curate, who was perhaps dining with his squire at the time, and though a feeling of awe would creep over his unsophisticated mind at beholding (through the medium, possibly, of two or three glasses of sherry) the lineal descendant, as he fondly imagined, of that very Robertus Latronus whose name figured at the top of the family tree,—yet, in the ears of the older and more knowing portion of the. community, this boasting of his pedigree savoured strongly of the ludicrous. However, Sir John was, for all that, a firm believer in his own pretensions, and as completely ignored the existence of his great grandfather, who was a surgeon-apothecary in a very small way in Newchurch (a few old people could *just* remember him), as if there never had been any such person. And he accordingly clung to the De Marburys, and dilated upon their exploits, just as if their red blood, and not the puddle of the surgeon-apothecary, trickled through his veins.

Except for this weakness—a pardonable one after all—Sir John was likely to make his way, and rise in the estimation of his brother squires and of people generally. He went in for all the county honours, picked up a smattering of law from the newspapers, and, after a time, presided occasionally, with some credit too, at quarter sessions in the absence of old Lord Powderham. He was a favourite with the barristers, who were glad to be asked out to dine at Donnington, and sometimes even to spend a day or two there. So they winked at any slips Sir John might make in his law, and, with one consent, while skirmishing with each other as usual, treated the chairman with unvarying respect, and helped him out of his little difficulties. And it was to some extent the same at agricultural dinners: Sir John, after he came of age, was in great request as chairman. He had some humour about him, and could throw off the little speeches expected on such occasions in a highly satisfactory manner. It was only when he came to real business matters—to pronouncing his opinion *ex cathedrâ* upon short horns and long horns, upon broad-breasted beasts and narrow-breasted, upon the best way of making cheese, and the like—that he found himself in a hobble. The farmers were by no means so complaisant as the barristers, and it only required for the chairman to drop a word in favour of short

horns to have all the long horns (speaking meta-
phorically) thrust on all sides of him : the broad-
breasters would be down upon him with indignation for his panegyric upon the narrow-breasts.
And as for Sir John (who, as new to the thing,
rather prided himself upon giving advice to the
farmers) venturing to find fault with the way in
which the Cheshire dairymaids made their cheese,
or in which the farmers cultivated their land, why,
poor Sir John had better have kept his well-meant
advice to himself.   For forthwith, upon one occasion in particular, there arose such a tremendous
hubbub on all sides, such storms of hisses and
cat-calls, and other such sounds which never fall
gratefully upon a speaker's ear, that, though
obliged to weather it all out, and even to appear
amused by it, yet it is believed that it was upon
that memorable occasion Sir John registered a
vow never again to seek to illumine the darkened
minds of Cheshire farmers, but to leave them to
their own ignorance and bad farming for the
future.   And there is some reason to suppose, too,
that he kept to his resolution ; for it was observed

that he was ever afterwards remarkably shy of
offering advice at mixed agricultural meetings in
his own county.   With this exception—when the
young squire, upon more than one occasion, would
have done well to have called to mind, and to
have acted upon, a certain well-known Latin
maxim, which implies that everybody is *supposed*
to understand his own business best—all went well
with him : he was becoming generally popular in
the county; his reign had opened auspiciously ; and
so here we leave him for the present, and turn to
others who are to figure in this history.

## CHAPTER II.

AND now to go back a little to Sir John's father. When it was understood that young Richard Hibbert was engaged to be married to the Honourable Elizabeth Simeon, Lord Clapham's eldest daughter, he was rallied a good deal by the county wits upon his choice of a " saint " as his wife. Not that anything particular was known of the young lady either one way or another, either for or against her. She was, indeed, too young at the time of her engagement for her character to be formed. But then she came of a very " strict family," and it seemed to be quite a matter of course that every one bearing the name of Simeon should be very Evangelical and Low Church. Nor was this notion entirely dispelled until the eldest son and

heir to the title astonished the world one day by
turning Roman Catholic, and ever afterwards dis-
playing an extraordinary degree of bitterness
against his former co-religionists, and especially
that particular section of them of which his father
continued to be the honoured and influential
leader.

Lady De Marbury brought with her to her husband's house all the traditions amongst which she
had been brought up.    Her father had been the
friend and adviser of Wilberforce and Thornton;
and the peculiar tenets which are identified with
their names represented to her mind the only
vital religion in existence.    How Miss Simeon or
her parents ever came to view with any degree
of favour such a wild, rattling, good-natured young
fellow as Dick Hibbert was a puzzle to many.
Nor was it quite easy to see what attractions the
young lady possessed in her lover's eyes; for she
was homely-looking enough, always dressed without taste, and brought but little fortune with her.
She had, however, prudence, and a fair share of
common sense—two qualities in which Sir Richard

was woefully deficient. And then the connection
was a good one, and it was not long before Lord
Clapham exerted his considerable political influence
in obtaining a revival of the baronetcy in favour
of his son-in-law, who had just changed his name
of Hibbert for De Marbury. Altogether, there
was less disparity about the alliance than seemed
at first sight: on one side, a title, a good income,
and a fine place situated in one of the most desirable parts of Cheshire; on the other, a respectable
connection, and a good position in society. Richard
Hibbert, too, though careless and reckless enough
in his habits, and devoted to field-sports, yet was
not wanting in affection for his wife, and readily
fell in with any of her little plans for promoting
the spiritual welfare of the tenantry or improving
the education of their children. Accordingly,
school-houses were built on the estate at her
instance, and efficient masters and mistresses provided. But what Lady De Marbury prized more
than anything else, and which was only brought
about by her own persevering efforts, was the
erection by her husband of a plain-looking edifice,

c

which was to serve as a church for the use of the
tenants and others who might choose to resort to it
in preference to the parish church of Donnington,
which was situated about a mile and a half from
the Hall.

This chapel, which was in a corner of the
demesne, and which appeared to have been
built after the model of a meeting-house, was only
licensed, not consecrated; so that, as Sir Richard
used sometimes to say, by way of a boast, and
her ladyship by way of a kind of threat levelled
at the rector, it might any day be diverted to
some other purpose—a barn, for instance, or a
Dissenting meeting-house. This chapel was a con-
tinual bone of contention between Sir Richard, or
rather Lady De Marbury, and the rector, Mr.
Hulton, then a young man. From the very first
her ladyship had expressed dissatisfaction with the
minister whom she found in possession at Donnington; and this dissatisfaction kept increasing until
it displayed itself openly in the erection, within
the demesne, of a chapel for the use of the Hall
family and tenantry. First it was Mr. Hulton's

" worldliness " that was complained of, and his frequent appearance at the Newchurch assemblies, where he attracted Lady De Marbury's unfavourable observation upon the only occasion, soon after his marriage, that she could be induced, at her husband's earnest entreaty, to favour that resort of county fashion with her presence ; and when, in course of time, Mr. Hulton married and " settled," and began to take up with " High Church notions," and to introduce frequent choral services, and to preach in his surplice, and to keep saints' days, it was then that Lady De Marbury's indignation boiled over. And it is not too much to say that the appearance of the surplice in Donnington pulpit was what gave the final and strongest impetus to the erection of the family chapel. Lady De Marbury gave her husband no peace until the building was set about ; and, as everything was to be " as plain as possible," at the special instance of Lord Clapham, who, as well as different members of his family, was a frequent visitor at Donnington Hall, it was not long before the edifice was completed, and the chapel ready to be " opened." A

delay, indeed, occurred in consequence of the
rector's determined hostility to the opening of
what he foresaw would be a regular opposition
place of worship in his parish ; and many and
disagreeable were the letters which passed between
him and Sir Richard on the subject. The Bishop's
interference was invoked by both parties. He was
a timorous man, and for some time endeavoured to
effect a compromise between them. His religious
sympathies were, indeed, all with the Hall people,
and, besides, he had a particular dislike to falling out with any of the "county families." But
then he could not very well throw the rector over-
board, who, he knew, had law and usage on his
side. So he vainly endeavoured to induce Sir
Richard and Lady De Marbury to allow the rector
to nominate a minister to the chapel, he also un-
dertaking to pay the stipend. But this was refused point-blank, and with something like contempt. It then came down to, might the rector
have a veto in the appointment? This was also
refused, and most decidedly. Things were now
at a dead lock, and Mr. Hulton and his wife, who

was quite as strong a partisan on her husband's side of the question as Lady De Marbury was on the opposite side, began to flatter themselves that the day was theirs, that the "Clapham faction" were defeated. But they little knew her ladyship, or the resources which her noble father (who had been the secret adviser throughout) had to fall back upon (if everything else failed), sooner than yield to their "High Church" rector. Accordingly, a studiously civil intimation was sent to the Bishop that it was Sir Richard De Marbury's intention to have the chapel that he had built licensed as a Dissenting meeting-house. This effected what, perhaps, nothing else would. Mr. Hulton shrunk with horror at the idea of a meeting-house within the very park, and of so many of his people being encouraged to declare themselves Dissenters; so that, at the Bishop's urgent request, he withdrew his opposition; and thus Donnington Chapel was duly licensed for public worship, "according to the rites and ceremonies of the United Church of England and Ireland." The great thing now was to get a "popular preacher," and (though such a thing was never named, yet it must have been uppermost in her ladyship's mind all along) to "empty the parish church;" and then Lady De Marbury's triumph over the rector and his wife would be complete.

In the meantime that care which her ladyship took of the morals of the people about her, and the vigilant supervision which she exercised (each year more strictly) over their affairs in general, might with great advantage have been brought to bear upon her husband and *his* concerns. Poor Dick De Marbury (as he was generally called) made no pretensions to religion. He, perhaps, thought that his wife possessed a supererogation of it which might be of avail to himself. At any rate, he was the best of husbands in leaving her alone, to be as religious as ever she liked, and to eschew balls and Newchurch assemblies to the end of her days, and he found her money for all her pet plans and projects. But then it was pretty clearly understood that he was not to be interfered with himself. He was to hunt, and shoot, and fish, to his heart's content. He liked, too, to have his house full of company of one kind or another. Even old Lord

Clapham, he would say, with his long extempore prayers, both morning and evening, and his endless preaching, even *he* was better than nobody. Altogether, Sir Richard pursued a somewhat reckless course, living much above his income (as was discovered when it was too late), and constantly making extravagant purchases of land; and, if his peccadilloes of another sort did not create any public scandal, it is to be feared that a dread of offending his rigidly proper wife, and her highborn connections, contributed very materially to the outward appearance of decorum which Sir Richard invariably maintained. However, the end was not long in coming. Comparatively young as he was, yet early dissipation and "living hard," in the frequent company of his sporting companions, cut short poor Dick's days in his thirty-first year: he was carried off in a few days by gastric fever, and a hatchment over the door of Donnington Hall, and a long inscription, setting forth all his virtues, followed by a text of Scripture, beautifully executed on a marble slab in Donnington Church, were very soon all that remained to remind people of poor Dick De Marbury.

The grief of persons of Lady De Marbury's character is usually not very intense. She quietly took it for granted that her husband was in heaven —a happy inconsistency—for, if only one-half of that which her favourite preacher at the chapel dinned into people's ears, Sunday after Sunday, was true, when he apparently consigned nine-tenths of mankind to eternal perdition, it is to be feared that poor Dick's *habitat* was not exactly where his fond wife placed it. However, such reflections did not seem to trouble Lady De Marbury. She dwelt complacently upon the many schools and churches which her deceased husband had contributed towards— and especially upon that one crowning act of his life, the erection of Donnington Chapel, and the anxiety he had always expressed that his tenants and servants should be regular in their attendance at church; and so she arrived at the comfortable conclusion that, under an apparent carelessness and even boyishness of demeanour, there was laid up a store of deep religious feeling and conscientiousness in her late husband's bosom which, had his life only been prolonged, would no doubt have developed itself and borne much fruit.

Consoled by such reflections, her ladyship devoted herself to looking into her deceased husband's affairs, and to the care and bringing-up of her only child, then a boy of ten or eleven. Averse to public schools, and from an unwillingness to lose sight of her child, Lady De Marbury was glad to turn to account the classical abilities of Mr. Hulton's curate, and to intrust young Sir John to his tuition. Accordingly, every morning, except Sundays, the lad might be seen trotting across the park upon his pony and making for the curate's lodgings, near the church. Sir Richard's early and unlooked-for death had done something towards healing the breach between the Hall and the Rectory. He had always been partial to Mr. Hulton, as his widow would mention in conversation, alleging it as an instance of Sir Richard's great goodness of heart and forgiving disposition. And, though irritated at the time at what he considered the rector's vexatious opposition to his

wishes in the matter of the chapel, yet, for some
time before his death, he had resumed his attendance of an afternoon at the parish church, and had
even made some overtures towards a reconciliation
with the rector and his wife.

" Hang it !" Sir Richard used sometimes to say
to one of his sporting companions; "why ever
did Hulton go and run counter to my Lady?
There, there is a stop put to all our intercourse.
And I used to like Hulton to come up and dine
here, and to have a chat with him.   And there is
his wife too—a prettier, nicer, brighter little
thing I don't know anywhere!  They are as
different as chalk is from cheese from that groan-
ing, cadaverous-looking fellow and  his vulgar
wife that we have got at our chapel here.   It
was that precious father-in-law of mine who sent
them here.  I only wish I had caught a sight of
the fellow's phiz before I engaged him.   And
then he preaches such tremendously long sermons,
and drops his _h_'s and all that sort of thing.  He
is a literate, or something of that sort; and we
can never have him at table when there is any one

staying here. As for his wife, happily we are spared *that* infliction."

In this way used Sir Richard to run on; and it must be admitted that, down to the time of his death, the chapel had not quite fulfilled his or Lady De Marbury's expectations. The sort of men who came there were decidedly not desirable. And then there were such frequent changes. The position of the minister of the chapel, or the chaplain, as he was sometimes called, was an awkward one. He had no cure of souls—had no right, strictly speaking, to visit ministerially in the parish, or to perform any other clerical office whatever outside the walls of his little chapel. And then the rector, Mr. Hulton, kept a very sharp eye upon the Hall chaplain and his doings, and would by no means, if he could possibly help it, permit the allegiance of his flock to be tampered with. He was, therefore, now more than doubly assiduous in his pastoral visiting, and would look up absentees from church with untiring energy. Besides, being a man of good family, and having been for so many years rector of the parish, and therefore well known to every one, he had manifestly a considerable advantage over those nameless individuals who from time to time filled the office of chaplain at Donnington Hall. Altogether, the position of the chaplain was not an enviable one. So things went on during Sir Richard's lifetime. And when, some time after his death, Lady De Marbury made an effort to secure the services of some one superior to the general run of those who had been hitherto officiating at the chapel, her object being that her chaplain should also act as tutor to her son, and be a companion for him, the result was not happy. For the new chaplain, a native of the sister isle, and fresh from Trinity College, Dublin, did not exactly combine the qualifications she looked for in her chaplain. He was a great deal too young and inexperienced, she thought, to prove a useful tutor for her son. And then he spoke with a strong Irish accent which grated upon her ladyship's fastidious ears. However, he soon made himself at home, and became a prodigious favourite with the little baronet, and popular

with the servants. He was a tall, handsome, good-
looking young fellow, with a pair of most un-
clerical black whiskers, and with brilliant dark
eyes, which the housemaid, Betty, declared were
"beauties." His sermons, too, delivered with all
the national fire, were greatly admired. "Not
much in them, certainly," Lady De Marbury
would say confidentially to her friends, "and too
many flowers and figures of speech for my fancy ;
but still people like them : they are more rousing
and energetic than poor Mr. Thomas's ; and, altogether, I suppose we must be satisfied. He is
very young too, and I suppose will improve as he
gets older."

But what commended him most in her ladyship's eyes was the uncommon fancy that her son,
young Sir John, seemed to have taken to the new
chaplain. They were inseparables ; and young
MacMahon—that was the chaplain's name—being
very strong and active, and expert at various out-
of-door games, won the admiration of all. Even the
rector called on him, and asked him to dinner ; and
both he and Mrs. Hulton could not but be amused

at their guest's native drollery and good-humour.
He was certainly very different from all his predecessors at the chapel.   Lady De Marbury did
not know what to think of it, and could not make
up her mind whether she liked the new chaplain
or not.   He was rather volatile, she thought; and
then her father didn't approve of him, that was
plain, and seldom even spoke to him when staying
at Donnington.   But this may have been prejudice;
and he was getting an old man now; and perhaps
he thought that Mr. MacMahon did not treat him
with sufficient respect.   So her ladyship thought
she would let things go on as they were; only she
hoped that her son was learning something.   She
was afraid that he did not look up to his tutor
enough.   She would consult the rector about it.
In the meantime the chaplain was becoming quite
paternal in his feelings towards his little pupil,
and loaded him with presents.   He would pat him
on the head, and bid him be a good boy, and he
would always have a friend in Tom MacMahon.
It began to be noticed, too, that the chaplain was
more for giving his opinion to the steward and

gardener, and people about the place, than he had
been.  He even once countermanded the cutting
down of a favourite tree—a piece of interference,
however, which he never attempted to repeat after
the blowing-up he got from the Scotch steward,
who was a Presbyterian, and disliked all parsons
except those of his own persuasion.  MacMahon
was too good-humoured to bear ill-will against the
man ; so he only laughed at him, and called him
" a crusty old fellow."   About this time, too—for
it all got well talked of afterwards—the chaplain's
sermons became more than ever poetical and
incomprehensible.   Scraps of paper, too, in his
handwriting, and containing long extracts from
Moore and Byron, would be found lying about the
house, and would turn up at odd times and places.
Sometimes they would flutter out of books which
Lady De Marbury was in the habit of reading, or
make their appearance between the leaves of the
drawing-room blotting-book, at which her ladyship
wrote most of her notes.   It was some time before
Lady De Marbury could in the least understand
these scraps of paper, when she attempted to read the

first few lines of them; for farther she never went. She had never heard of Moore in her life, much less read any of his profane poetry; and as for Byron, she only knew him as a Lord, and a very wicked one too, who was separated from his wife, and had written a great deal that was objectionable. As for any chaplain of hers, who had the unlimited *entrée* of the house, being an admirer of such a character, or of his writings, such a dreadful thought would never be likely to cross her ladyship's mind. She had no taste for poetry herself, except in the shape of hymns, and could never understand people—serious people too—admiring what usually struck her as a farrago of nonsense. When such scraps of paper thus turned up, it never entered Lady De Marbury's mind to attach any importance to them. She never read them beyond the first line or two; but, perceiving them to be in rhyme, and in her chaplain's handwriting, she came to the conclusion, they were written so carefully, that he was endeavouring to improve his hand, none of the best at any time; or possibly they were, she thought, "nonsense-verses," of which

she remembered to have heard something in her
school-room days, and designed probably for the
instruction of her son. She never attached the
slightest personal meaning to the verses; and
accordingly, when her eye happened to light upon

"Come to my bosom, my own stricken deer!"

in the chaplain's handwriting, it never occurred
to her that the "stricken deer" was that great,
tall, black-whiskered young fellow whom she
encountered twenty times a day in one place or
another, and that the invitation was supposed to
issue from her own matronly lips. However,
things went on as usual for a time, the chaplain
seeking in vain for signs of consciousness in Lady
De Marbury's countenance; when, upon a week-
day evening, after there had been the usual once-
a-week service in the chapel, and after a sermon
delivered with more than usual energy, the chaplain resolved to declare his passion, which he had
persuaded himself needed only *to be* declared in
order to ensure an ardent return; and so, taking
advantage of a quiet half-hour when the servants

D

had gone to supper, and after Sir John had retired
for the night (he said he was going to bed shortly,
but he first paid a visit to the harness-room, where
he was taking lessons in smoking from one of the
stable-helpers), thus, choosing his opportunity,
and speaking in a very weak, fluttering voice, poor
MacMahon disclosed to the widow the meaning of
all those mysterious scraps of paper which had so
long puzzled her; drew attention to his own
altered looks, as evidence of the sincerity of his
passion; and finally, as not a word fell all the time
from the lady, made a vain attempt to possess
himself of her hand, while he devoted himself
heart and soul to her future happiness, if she
would accept him, and thereby make him the
happiest of men. Poor Mac (as his friends familiarly called him) had never a very clear idea,
when he recurred to the subject, as he frequently
did in after times, as to what the widow actually
*did* say to him on this occasion. He had only a
vague recollection of her angrily drawing away
her hand, and pushing back her chair, and saying
something about his having lost his senses, to be

guilty of such impertinence, and then of a hurried movement towards the bell, and then of finding himself in the hall, and of letting himself out of the door before the servant who had been rung for had time to come and be a witness to his disgrace. Poor MacMahon's thoughts were none of the clearest as he made his way through the shrubbery on that moonlight night towards his farm-house lodgings, at a little distance off. "What ever *is* to be done?" he found himself saying twenty times in the course of that night and the following morning. However, he was not long left in doubt. "A servant from the Hall, sir, has brought this letter," said the woman who waited on him—the farmer's wife—"and please, sir, he says he is to take back a receipt."

"Very well, Mrs. Clarke. Let him wait for a minute; I will tell you when it is ready." A thin, coloured piece of paper of an oblong shape fell from the opened letter. It was a cheque upon Messrs. Jones, Loyd, and Co., of Manchester, for the amount of a quarter's salary in advance. This told its own tale plainly enough. There were but two or three lines written on a sheet of note-paper.

"Lady De Marbury encloses Mr. MacMahon a quarter's salary in advance, and has no further occasion for his services.

"Donnington Hall, Oct. 184—."

"Poor Mac, I am sorry you are going," cried out the little baronet, bursting into the room soon after Mr. MacMahon's receipt of the letter; "and we are all sorry for you—the servants, and all; they have been just telling me so; and Jack Tomlinson says he will put the horse into the trap any time you want it, and drive you to the station. You wanted to marry mamma, I hear. But that wouldn't do, you know. And they are all saying, in the servants' hall, how mad grandpapa will be with you when he hears of it; and he is coming down to-day by the mail-train."

"Well, good-bye, my boy," said MacMahon, with an attempt at cheerfulness; "your mother needn't have been so hard on me, and talked about it, as she seems to have done."

"Oh, everybody knows it by this time. 'Bye, 'bye, Mac;" and off scampered the young baronet to tell his mamma "how awfully cut up old Mac seemed to be." Poor MacMahon's arrangements were soon made. A carpet-bag and portmanteau —to follow him to the station—contained all his worldly goods. His landlady was settled with; her husband was called out of the field; then there was a general shaking of hands and wishing of good-byes and "God bless you's;" and so the Rev. Thomas MacMahon turned his back with a sore heart enough upon the pleasant woods and green fields of Donnington Hall.

## CHAPTER III.

AFTER this little affair of Mr. MacMahon's, which
the widow talked of quite openly and with considerable bitterness, there was an interregnum
at the chapel for some time, and the duty
was taken by the master of the grammar-school
at Newchurch.   An arrangement was next made
with Mr. Hulton that he should allow one of his
curates to officiate occasionally.   And so, one way
or another, the services were kept up.   And thus
things remained until within about a year of the
coming of age of Sir John.   It so happened then
that an application for the chaplaincy, from one
the Rev. Paul Marshall, reached Lady De Marbury through the medium of a "Christian friend,"
who had heard Mr. Marshall highly spoken of in

Brighton a year or two previously. Mr. Marshall had only just lately returned from abroad, where he had been, it was understood, for the benefit of his health. He was a middle-aged man, Lady De Marbury's friend informed her, of gentlemanly manners, and no doubt a graduate of one of the Universities. Altogether, Lady De Marbury liked what she heard of him ; and, as her son was now emancipated from tutors and governors, there was all the less difficulty in making a proper selection of a chaplain. A visit from Mr. Marshall himself confirmed her ladyship's favourable impressions. He was evidently a man who had mixed in society. His address was particularly bland and insinuating. He had been on the Continent for some time, and, while at Rome, had seen a good deal, he said, of Lady De Marbury's eldest brother, who now, by the death of his father, was Lord Clapham, and of whose awful "perversion" Mr. Marshall spoke in the strongest and most affecting terms. In person Mr. Marshall, whose age appeared to be forty, was about the middle height, and sparely made. He was dark, and of a sallow,

bilious complexion. His appearance was not what
would be considered prepossessing; but yet, when
he spoke, there was something rather attractive
and pleasing in his manner. He expressed himself on the theological subjects of the day in a
manner which delighted Lady De Marbury, and
strongly reminded her, she said, of her dear friend
Daniel Wilson, formerly of Islington, now Bishop
of Calcutta. Mr. Marshall was for no half-
measures. "If I come to Donnington," he would
say, "my great aim and effort must be to root
out Tractarianism from the place. It is far more
dangerous than downright Popery. When you
have got to do with a Romanist you have got to
do with an open enemy; but when it is with a
Tractarian, you see before you a concealed traitor,
one who hasn't the courage or honesty to show
his real colours. So I tell your ladyship fairly
that, if I come to Donnington, there must be no
paltering, as far as I am concerned, with Popery
in disguise. I shall consider it my bounden duty
to endeavour to open Sir John's eyes to the pernicious teaching and practices of these Tractarians,

and to preserve him in the simplicity of the Protestant faith." Lady De Marbury could have
taken Mr. Marshall in her arms and absolutely
hugged him, if such a thing had been at all
proper in a grave, staid matron like herself, she
was so delighted with the sentiments he expressed.
Here was the very man she had been so long on
the look-out for—a polished, gentlemanly, and
educated man, who would be something of a match
for Mr. Hulton. He appeared to have the Romish
controversy quite at his finger-ends, and to entertain a perfect abhorrence both of Popery and
Tractarianism. "It may be bad taste in me,"
he said, "but I have no sympathy with your
gaudily decorated churches, with your handsome
stained windows, surpliced choristers, and all the
'man-millinery' that is now the rage. Give
me the plain, simple Protestant service of our
Reformers, and an unpretending structure like
that yonder in the park, and I ask no more."
Lady De Marbury, as we have said, was quite
delighted with her visitor, and wrote off at once
to her friend Miss Cecil at Brighton, to thank her

for sending them such a treasure.  Sir John did
not testify the same admiration of Mr. Marshall.
He always preferred the parish church, and its
choral services, to their own uninteresting chapel,
and the long sermons usually delivered there.
But this, as Mr. Marshall quietly observed to
Lady De Marbury, was only what might be expected.  Sir John had been too long exposed to
the insidious snares of Tractarianism.  It must
be his (Mr. Marshall's) endeavour to open his
eyes.  No doubt to the natural man there was
something very alluring in all these ceremonies
and decorations and will-worship.

"Let us hope, my dear lady," said Mr. Marshall,
taking her ladyship's hand, "that we may be
able to replace them with something better.  For
truly I feel an interest in your son already, and
would gladly help to rescue him from the snare of
the fowler."

Lady De Marbury and Mr. Marshall then
parted, mutually satisfied with each other.  Sir
John was too young, and had been too long accustomed to his mother's sway, to think of offering

any opposition to her choice of a chaplain. He
only hoped that something or other would occur to
defeat it, and in the meantime resigned himself to
his fate. But in due time Mr. Marshall did arrive
and was duly installed in the lodgings usually
occupied by the chaplain. Here let us leave him
for the present, and turn to another individual
whose name has hitherto been only casually introduced—the Rev. Peter Delawney, the Roman
Catholic priest. The De Marbury family had
always been Roman Catholics down to Sir Thomas,
the father of Sir Hugh, the last of the old line, and
he was the first who conformed to the Church of
England—more, it was thought, because the obnoxious religion which he professed was a barrier
to his promotion in the army than from any con-
scientious convictions. But, however this might
be, the son, Sir Hugh, was brought up in the re-
formed faith, and the property had ever since
remained in Protestant hands. One memorial,
however, remained at Donnington, or, we might
rather say, two, to keep up the recollection of what
had been once the family faith, and that for so

many generations; and this was a small Roman
Catholic chapel, which stood at no great distance
from the house, and forming part of a still older
building, once the residence of the family, which
had fallen into decay, and was now only kept up
as a sort of picturesque ruin. To this chapel there
was attached a priest whose stipend formed a charge
upon the Donnington estate. His congregation
was not a large one; it consisted of a few of the
middle-class tradespeople in Newchurch, with a
sprinkling of Irish labourers who were employed
on the adjacent farms. Occasionally, too, some
Roman Catholic gentleman, or a foreigner
stopping in the neighbourhood, would attend the
service. And it was in Father Delawney's power
to boast that Prince This and Count That had often
formed a member of his little congregation when
staying at the Hall or elsewhere. It had always
been an object with the Roman Catholic authorities
to win back the De Marburys, if possible, to the
ancient faith, and therefore they had always been
particular as to the priest assigned for the Donnington mission. It was necessary that he should

be a gentleman, in order to obtain admission to
the squire's table. It was necessary that he
should be a man of some parts, in order to be able
to cope with the Protestant rector, whom he would
often probably meet at the Hall, and be liable to
be brought in collision with at any time. He
must not be too strict—that is, he must be something of a man of the world—or he might only
disgust and give offence where he ought to try and
conciliate. And, lastly, he must have zeal and
energy, and never lose sight of the main object of
his mission—the recovery of the De Marburys to
the Catholic faith. All along this object had been
perseveringly pursued, and with some share of
success. Old Sir Thomas De Marbury, the father
of Sir Hugh, had, upon his death-bed, it is said,
been "reconciled to the Church" by the Abbé Le
Grand, who was at that time the priest of Donnington. Of Sir Hugh it would have been difficult to say what religion he belonged to. For,
after the marriage of his sister with Dr. Hibbert,
which he violently resented at the time, Sir Hugh
ceased to attend the parish church, or any other

church; and, in fact, he never entered Donnington Church again until brought there to be laid with his ancestors. So that, though he never formally abjured his religion, yet he could scarcely be claimed as a member of the Anglican Church, whose services he habitually absented himself from. But for his sudden death, occasioned by an accident while out hunting, the Abbé Le Grand always maintained that, like his father, he would have returned to the old faith of his family before his death had time been allowed. And it is certain that, upon the strength of this, masses were offered up for his soul in the little chapel, and even an effort made, which was fiercely and successfully resisted by little Dr. Hibbert, the rector, to bury the deceased baronet with the rites and ceremonies of the Roman Catholic Church. Any attempts to change the faith of Richard Hibbert (to whom the property, contrary to all expectation, had been willed by Sir Hugh) would have been utterly useless. In the first instance, by his father, and subsequently by his rigid Calvinistic wife, poor Dick was a great deal too closely watched and

taken care of for any priest to have the remotest
chance of gaining him over as a convert. Mr.
Delawney, who had succeeded the Abbé Le Grand,
was obliged, therefore, to confine himself to making
occasional allusions to the ancient faith of the
De Marburys, and to uttering half-jocular prophecies that Sir Richard would have to send for
him some time or other. But further than this he
durstn't go. Lady De Marbury had, in fact, given
him plainly to understand that, if he wished to
remain on friendly terms with the family, his attempts at proselytizing must cease, and the Father
had deemed it wisest to take the hint and bide
his time. It is true that, soon after her ladyship's
coming to the Hall, each party had made an attempt to convert the other. The priest had wil-
lingly promised to read some of the Clapham tracts
which her ladyship had brought from home with
her, and had even professed to be struck with some
of her own arguments. But, when he came to seek
reciprocity, to ask for a patient consideration for
his own little books, including the Rosary and
" Garden of the Soul," and said something about

having invoked the Blessed Virgin's intercession in behalf of Lady De Marbury, all expectations vanished on either side, and each party, from that time forth, looked upon the other as a hopeless subject for conversion.

From many little hints which Mr. Delawney dropped, it was evident that, though the father had slipped through his hands, and though it was clear enough that nothing was to be made of the mother, yet that of the son's conversion he had considerable hopes. It was at a time when many adverse decisions against the doctrines and faith of the Church of England, as it was thought, were being given in the courts of law; and High Church squires and catholic-minded young ladies would talk of quitting a communion thus seriously compromised as respected its articles of faith, and of setting up some kind of church for themselves, after the fashion of the non-jurors. Amongst the persons who took up this cry—he was in the habit of hearing the subject frequently discussed at the Rectory—was young Sir John. It has been said that he had rather a weakness for being considered

one of the old stock—a regular De Marbury; and, as
they might be said to have been all Roman Catholics, he certainly entertained no particular antipathy
himself towards the faith of his "ancestors." He
was keen enough, too, to perceive—or at least he
fancied he perceived—something like inconsistency
between Mr. Hulton's avowed opinions upon many
subjects, especially the sacraments, and his love of
ceremonies, and his general mode of conducting
the Church service, all strongly savouring of
Popery—at least Sir John thought so—and the
downright hostility he always exhibited towards
Roman Catholics themselves and their faith. He
and Mr. Delawney were hardly on speaking
terms; indeed, they never conversed, except at
Sir John's table, when occasionally, especially
after the arrival of Mr. Marshall, theological or
ecclesiastical subjects would come upon the *tapis*.
Mr. Delawney always spoke of the rector as a very
high kind of gentleman, and as scorning a "poor
priest" like himself; while Mr. Hulton in return
looked upon the priest as a "deep, designing
Jesuit," which he probably was. If Sir John's

E

own tendencies, and the remarks he was in the
habit of hearing made, not only at the rector's
table, but also at the different county houses where
he stayed—if these all led him to look with no very
unfavourable eye upon the little ivy-covered
chapel, with its simple cross, and on the services
which were performed there, it is to be feared that
the highly Calvinistic discourses which he had to
listen to on Sunday mornings at his own chapel
did nothing to counteract those influences.    It
was always bad enough, Sir John used to say,
as regarded most of his mother's chaplains, and
the occasional helps, whom he could remember;
but nothing ever equalled the fanaticism which
poured from the lips of the last arrival—the Rev.
Paul Marshall.  By his account the Pope was
Antichrist, the Church of Rome the Scarlet
Woman sitting upon the seven hills, and the
Tractarians, whom he never lost sight of, and for
whom indeed he reserved his deadliest blows, were
the "frogs," referred to in the book of Revela-
tion, which "came out of the mouth of the
dragon, and out of the mouth of the beast, and

out of the mouth of the false prophet." Upon this subject—and, as he was an extempore preacher, it was a subject which seemed to find its way into every sermon he preached—Mr. Marshall would become perfectly frantic, and his pale saturnine features would appear to be lighted up with an almost unearthly expression. Lady De Marbury would listen to his words with rapt attention, and seem to hang upon the preacher's lips. She would glance occasionally at her son to see what effect such impassioned words were producing upon him. But nothing was to be read in Sir John's countenance but sheer amazement at the preacher's violence, and at the strange applications of Scripture in which he indulged. All his fire, all his energy, seemed to be reserved for the sermon. The prayers he read through in a slovenly, listless manner, as though going through some irksome task; and, as a prayer-meeting invariably followed each service, which he conducted with warmth and energy enough, it might be naturally concluded that, in Mr. Marshall's estimation, the Church's prayers were insufficient of

themselves to convey all that a true worshipper
must needs express.    With these prayer-meetings,
of course, Sir John had nothing to do, though his
lady mother much approved of them, and was one
of the most regular attendants.    But often on a
Sunday, in crossing the park, after he had been
listening for upwards of an hour to Mr. Marshall's
wild fanatical effusions, would Sir John heave a
sigh as he called to mind those solemn chants and
strains of music which on every seventh morning
would come wafted over the mere which lay between the Roman Catholic chapel and his own
house.

## CHAPTER IV.

WE have not as yet described the Rev. Father
Delawney. He was, then, a short, stout, good-
humoured-looking man, with rather a red face,
closely shaven, and with a merry twinkling gray
eye. He was very particular and natty about his
dress, and, but for the piece of white muslin round
his neck, might have been taken for some well-
endowed Protestant dignitary. For he always
wore one of those curiously-shaped hats, turned
up at the sides, much affected by deans and arch-
deacons and other great personages. In fact, the
Rev. Father *did* fill some dignified post in the
cathedral church of Chester, to which he said he
had been canonically inducted, though the duties
(and salary) of his office were in abeyance, and

likely, to all appearances, to remain so. However, this was enough to entitle him to be called amongst his own flock " Canon Delawney ;" and he would sometimes say humorously, when dining at the Hall, that he was entitled, by reason of his " Canon's stall," to take precedence of all the parsons present, instead of following in their wake as he generally did. But neither his titular dignity, nor his joke, could make any impression upon the rector, who would pass him unceremoniously, generally with Lady De Marbury on his arm, with the same air of indifference and non-recognition with which he would pass presently the servants who lined the Hall. Independently of any serious considerations, Mr. Delawney was not unacceptable to Sir John. His constant good-humour made him rather a favourite; and then he had been there so long, and had known Sir John ever since he had been a child. Apparently, too, there was no bigotry about him. He always spoke in a humorous, half-jesting way about the many divisions which existed amongst Protestants, and would casually contrast them with the union

and harmony which prevailed amongst "Catholics."
He would make a joke of the rector's dislike
towards himself, though they had been acquaint-
ances for so many years ; and, what rather took
Sir John's fancy, the priest would regularly, on
the first day of the hunting season, and on other
special occasions, seek out Sir John, and solemnly
give him his blessing. He would allege that such
had been always the custom at Donnington—which
was quite enough for Sir John—and so, though
half ashamed of his compliance, the young baronet
would partly kneel while the priest, with extended
hands, and in Latin, would implore the protection
of Heaven, and of all the saints there, upon the
head of the young man. "I am an old man compared with you," the priest would say kindly to
him, "and the blessings of an old man never
harmed any one yet."

From the circumstance of their respective resi-
dences being so near to each other, the priest and
Mr. Marshall were frequently meeting, especially
at the Hall. There appeared to be a kind of
armed peace between them. Mr. Marshall, of

course, always spoke of the other as being under
an "awful delusion," but seemed to accord him
that credit for sincerity which he withheld from
the rector and his party; while Father Delawney, protesting his desire to live peaceably
with all men—with the rector himself, if he
might be allowed—would good-humouredly discuss with Mr. Marshall, in the presence of Sir
John (to "keep the peace," as the priest would
pleasantly observe), the points of difference between the two Churches. The conversation, indeed, would often turn upon such subjects after
dinner, and Mr. Hulton, when present, would not
unfrequently be drawn into it. He had no liking
for discussing theological subjects at such a time
and in such company. But, in the presence of
startling assertions, he could not hold his peace;
and, unfortunately, he usually found himself
opposed to two adversaries, who, viewing the same
question from opposite extremes, yet agreed in
differing from the rector, and in condemning his
views. Mr. Marshall spoke well and fluently, and
had perfect command of his temper, so far at least

as to refrain from any actual intemperance of
expression. But he had that manner which
irritates an opponent perhaps more than violence
of language. He would speak with a calm
assumption of superiority, seeking to draw out
the other's meaning, and then, by putting some
extreme or ridiculous case, endeavour to amuse
the company at his expense. To one naturally
proud and reserved, like Mr. Hulton, and especially when on his own ground, as rector of the
parish, and in the presence of his leading parish-
ioner—sometimes Lady De Marbury would be
present as well—such a manner seldom failed to
be highly offensive to him; and he could not but
be aware of the bad effect which must be produced
upon the mind of a young man like Sir John at
seeing two clergymen of the same Church at such
hopeless variance from each other, and that, too,
upon really fundamental points. In his good-
humoured way, too, the priest would not be slow
to take advantage of the circumstance.

"When you two gentlemen," he would say,
"have settled between yourselves what is really

the doctrine of your own Church, it will be time enough for the poor Catholic priest to answer you."

"My dear Hulton, do you seriously tell me," Mr. Marshall said on one of these occasions, with a mingled tone of seriousness and irony, "that you attach any importance to the figment of apostolical succession? Why not be content to rest the foundation of our Protestant Church upon the faith of our martyred Reformers, instead of going back to the dark ages of superstition?"

"Do you mean to say," asked Mr. Hulton, rather hotly, "that you think the Church of England was founded at the Reformation? because, if you do——"

"Excuse me, Hulton. What possible advantage can it be to the cause of truth to trace up the spiritual ancestry of our bishops through a succession of Romish prelates? Even if the thing could be proved, which it can't, of what value would it be? Better rely for our credentials, as ministers of the Gospel, upon the authority of the 'written Word' than occupy our minds with fables and endless genealogies."

" Then, Mr. Marshall, do you consider there is any difference between a priest of the Church of England and a Dissenting minister ?"

" Priest ! I don't like the word ; minister is the more evangelical term. However, as to your question, I think, if a person is lawfully ' called by his congregation,' and if he preaches the truth, he is quite as much a minister as either you or I ; and you know that the 23rd Article says the same."

" Well, it is useless pursuing the subject," observed Mr. Hulton, with some displeasure.

" And then, if I might put in but one word," said the priest, " when you talk, Mr. Hulton, about the apostolical succession, you cannot have forgotten all about the Nag's Head controversy !"

" What was that, Father Peter ?" asked Sir John, who had been listening attentively to the conversation.

" Oh, he is only referring to the consecration of our first Protestant archbishop—Parker," said Mr. Marshall, with a smile. "I believe there was some little irregularity about it

—he consecrated himself, or something of that sort."

"You must be aware, Mr. Marshall," broke in the rector, angrily, as he was preparing to leave the room, "that the fable of the Nag's Head has been given up by Lingard, and by every respectable Roman Catholic writer."

"Well, well, what does it signify? As long as we preach the truth, we needn't trouble our heads about such things."

"It is sad to see your Church so disunited," observed Father Peter to Sir John as they remained behind the others over their wine.

"Yes, there *is* some difference between Hulton's preaching and Mr. Marshall's. You know I have to attend our own chapel on Sunday forenoons; my mother wishes it; but I like to go to the afternoon service at Donnington. And it is hard to know, between them both, what *is* really the faith of the Church of England."

"I should be sorry for it if I were one of you." This was the priest's answer; and here the conversation closed.

The above is but a slight specimen of the conversations that frequently passed at Sir John's table after Mr. Marshall's arrival; for, let Mr. Hulton have determined as he might not to be betrayed into taking any part in such passages of arms, which he was sure to repent of afterwards, yet, from his zeal and natural temperament, he was too often hurried into a defence of his principles, especially when assailed, either openly or covertly, by one from whom he might naturally have counted upon aid, and not opposition. Sir John had a turn for theology, and was interested rather than otherwise in hearing such subjects discussed; and as for Lady De Marbury, she was so persuaded of the advantage it must be to her son to be put on his guard against Tractarianism, that she heartily approved of, and seconded in every way, Mr. Marshall's endeavours frequently to give the conversation such a direction as to afford him an opportunity of declaring his sentiments. Such was the state of things at the Hall, and only a few months had elapsed since Sir John's coming of age, when a visit from

his uncle, Lord Clapham, was announced. Upon
the occasion of his lordship's last visit—then the
Hon. Richard Simeon—he had bidden fair to
tread in the steps of his father, of Exeter Hall
celebrity. He had had several battles with the
rector; had conducted much of the correspondence
with the bishop about the licensing of the little
chapel; had been a prime mover and director in
that business throughout; and, above all, had
made the most strenuous efforts to get rid of
Father Delawney and his chapel out of the
demesne. He not only refused to meet him at
dinner, or to be introduced to him, but distributed
tracts and publications in all directions, cautioning
people against Popery. Nay, his religious zeal
was carried so far that he refused to attend the
services at Donnington Church, but put himself
to the trouble of walking a considerable distance
every Sunday morning to another church. Now
all was changed; and Father Delawney had the
satisfaction of receiving a very humble epistle from
the noble convert, expressing the deepest sorrow
for his past refractory behaviour, and a desire to

perform some kind of public penance upon the
occasion of his approaching visit to Donnington.
This letter it was not safe to communicate at the
Hall : any publication of its contents might, by
causing the visit to be declined, have interfered
with the edifying little spectacle which Father
Delawney had in store for his people on the Sunday after the arrival of Lord Clapham.  It was, of
course, tacitly understood that his lordship (who
was a weak, delicate-looking young man) would
attend Father Delawney's little chapel on the
following morning; but certainly her ladyship
never calculated on the sight which actually met
her astonished view, and that of Sir John, almost
the first thing next day, as they stood at the
windows of the morning room, which commanded
a view of the little ivy-covered chapel with its
cross, on the other side of the mere.  At first their
attention was attracted by an unusual crowd about
the chapel, and very soon afterwards by a figure
clad in a white sheet, to be seen kneeling down
outside the porch, and remaining in that position
bareheaded, and upon a cold winter's morning.

A considerable time elapsed before the ruddy face
of Father Delawney presented itself. A total pros-
tration of the kneeling peer upon the cold stones
followed, and then some ceremony appeared to be
gone through, probably the absolution; and after
that it was evident that the risen peer was addressing the by-standers. Shortly afterwards the
whole party disappeared within the chapel, where
the peer served the priest at mass, it was soon
known. The penance scene was witnessed by
Lady De Marbury with burning cheeks; and
scarcely a word passed between herself and her
son during the entire time that the ceremony
lasted. It was not, however, quite finished yet.
A blazing fire, a little in front of the chapel, soon
attracted attention, and drew the party from the
breakfast-table to the windows again; and here
the sight that met the eye was no less astounding
than the other: it was a general burning of all
the books and tracts which his lordship, as Mr.
Simeon, had for years been in the habit of dis-
tributing amongst the people. The books and
tracts were delivered by the priest to his lordship,

who, with his own hands, tossed them into the flames. A visitor fresh from such an *auto-da-fé* could not, we might have thought, have been a very acceptable guest at Lady De Marbury's breakfast-table, even though that guest was her own brother; and probably he was not. But Lord Clapham's delicate appearance and unquestionable sincerity pleaded for indulgence; and, besides, her ladyship had a notable plan for reconverting him and bringing him back to the Protestant faith. She had consulted Mr. Marshall about it, who thought that the thing was possible. There could be no harm in trying, at any rate; and, with this view, and that they might see as much of each other as possible, Mr. Marshall was invited to be a visitor at the Hall during the entire time that Lord Clapham stayed, which was to be about a week.

## CHAPTER V.

LADY DE MARBURY had continued to reside at the
Hall after her son had attained his majority. She
had not been in the habit of seeing much company
herself, either during Sir Richard's lifetime, or
after she became a widow. Their principal visitors
would be relations and friends of the family. To
the clergy, too, connected with Donnington it
had been always customary to extend hospitality.
Things had not much altered since Sir John had
come of age. Every now and then two or three
of the neighbouring squires, with their wives and
daughters, would come to dinner, but nothing
more. Upon the occasion, however, of Lord Clapham's visit, being the first since his accession to
the title, and with a view of paying him a com-

pliment, two or three large parties were to be given, and several of the guests had been invited, not only to dine, but also to sleep. Mr. Marshall, as has been said, was amongst those who were to be staying in the house. This influx of visitors required a good deal of management as respected the rooms, in order that all parties might be suitably accommodated. In many instances dressing-rooms had to be provided as well. Altogether, there was some difficulty in deciding where the guests were to be bestowed. Lady De Marbury usually occupied one of the principal bed-rooms, which was over the dining-room; but upon this occasion she gave it up, with its adjacent dressing-room, to Lord and Lady Withington, who were to stay for a few days, and she had to take refuge in one of a cluster of small rooms which lay somewhat by themselves in a wing of the house. Here most of the single young men of the party were quartered, including Lord Clapham. Mr. Marshall, too, had one of these rooms assigned to him. The first grand party was given on the Tuesday after Lord Clapham's arrival. Some came

to dinner, such as Mr. and Mrs. Hulton, but most
of the guests were staying in the house. The
party broke up rather late for a country house;
and Lady De Marbury, with whose habits late
hours did not agree, was glad to slip away quietly
to her room as soon as Lady Withington and a
few of the principal ladies had retired for the
night. Presently, one after another was heard
coming up-stairs, and, with a friendly "good
night," going into their rooms. Every now and
then a loiterer would make his way up who had,
perhaps, been smoking a cigar down-stairs with
Sir John. But at length the last door seemed to
have been shut for the night, and then all was
still. Lady De Marbury was in the habit of sitting up reading for some time before she went to
bed, and upon this night, and after all the bustle
and excitement of the day, she especially enjoyed
the thoughts of a quiet half-hour with her Bible
and books of devotion. Accordingly, her maid
dismissed for the night, she composed herself to
read. The next room to hers was her brother's.
She could hear him moving about the room, stirring

the fire, and drawing up the blind. He was probably looking out of the window and admiring the
beautiful moonlight night. His eye would be
directed, no doubt, across the gleaming sheet of
water which lay before him, and would rest upon
those ivy-covered walls, the scene of his recent
penance. Lady De Marbury could have gone in
and thrown herself in her brother's arms, so deeply
was her heart touched with recollections of the past,
painful and otherwise, which were so intimately
interwoven with him. She recalled him as a
boy at school, at Westminster; she could remember very well when he was born, being
several years his senior, and the rejoicings which
took place on that event; and then his college
days, when he would stay for weeks together at
Donnington, during the hunting and shooting
seasons, and go out with Sir Richard. And then,
in after-times, when he had taken a serious turn,
and gave promise of treading in his father's steps,
and was looked upon as a young man of great
promise in the regions of Exeter Hall, his sister
would recall his frequent visits to her then

widowed house, and his youthful zeal and restless
activity, and incessant tract-distributing, and even
reading and lecturing in the cottages. And now
it seemed like a dreadful dream, something to
make their dead father turn in his coffin, to think
of the miserable scene of the Sunday previous: a
peer of England in a white sheet, kneeling before
a Romish priest, heaping words of scorn and contumely upon the faith in which he had been
brought up, and afterwards, by such a public
and significant act, expressing such utter hate and
detestation of those principles which he had formerly been so assiduous in propagating! Such
thoughts as these were crowding into Lady
De Marbury's mind as the simple footfall
sounded in her ear, and she had thoughts of
rushing in and imploring her brother, the bearer
of an honoured name and title, to listen to reasoning and advice—to allow Mr. Marshall to speak
with him; she would pray him, she thought,
for the sake of their common father's memory, to
return to his early faith. Lady De Marbury had
almost made up her mind to take this step, when

the stealthy turning of a handle in one of the adjoining rooms first attracted her notice and then excited her curiosity. It was from Mr. Marshall's room that the sound proceeded. Then, in a moment or two, a cautious footstep was heard to cross the passage, and there was a low knock at Lord Clapham's door. The person who knocked did not wait for the answer, but walked into the room like one who was expected, and the door was shut.

Lady De Marbury could not doubt but that the person who went into Lord Clapham's room was Mr. Marshall. The conversation was carried on in a low under-tone. Mr. Marshall seemed to be relating something, and there was a comment or observation occasionally from the other. A suppressed laugh fell uncomfortably on the listener's ears; it proceeded evidently from Mr. Marshall. "What can these two have to say to each other at this late hour of the night?" thought Lady De Marbury to herself. It could not be that Mr. Marshall had entered that night upon his task of seeking to win back his lordship to the faith. He would not

have chosen such a time and place for it, she knew.
Besides, though she could hardly detect a single
word that passed between them—only Mr. Hulton's
name once or twice reaching her ears—yet she
could tell that the tone was not a controversial one
—no eager questions and answers, no indignant
disclaimers, no impatient interruptions. It was
more that of a person relating a narrative, and
laughing occasionally at the humorous portions of
it. Lady De Marbury thought that the sitting
would never come to an end. There was no retiring
to rest until it was over. She was getting nervous
and fidgety; she could give no reason for it. Why
should not her brother and Mr. Marshall have a
little chat together before going to bed? Every
one did it—young ladies did it; where was the
harm? Her brother and Mr. Marshall had met
abroad; what so natural as that they should like to
talk over old times?

At length there were symptoms of a move in
the next room—a yawn and exclamation of fatigue
from her brother, and then a pushing back of
chairs from the fireplace, and then a pause of a

moment or two, and then the handle of the door was turned softly and Mr. Marshall came out. Lady De Marbury just overheard him saying, as he left, apparently with reference to something his lordship had said, "Why, you know everything is fair in war," and then the door was shut, and Mr. Marshall returned to his own room, so as scarcely to be heard.

Lady De Marbury could not get to sleep for some time. At length, taking it for granted that something must have passed between them both in former times, more than she was aware of— perhaps money transactions (Lord Clapham being wealthy)—her ladyship almost dismissed the subject from her mind. At breakfast, however, something occurring to remind her of it, she made the remark to her brother that he seemed to have been sitting up rather late the previous night. "For I slept in the next room to you," she added, carelessly, by way of accounting for the observation. Lord Clapham looked slightly confused for a moment, and, taking up a newspaper, merely remarked that he had not been aware they had been such near neighbours. Mr. Marshall, however, who was sitting opposite, explained everything, by saying to Lady De Marbury, with one of his most meaning looks, and in his blandest voice, that he and his lordship were " having a chat about old times ;" and so the subject was allowed to drop.

After this no particular intimacy was observable between Lord Clapham and Mr. Marshall. The conversation, however, after dinner, when there was no company, turned more than ever upon theological subjects. They were disembarrassed now of the presence of Mr. Hulton, who of late had invariably excused himself from making one of their family party, only dining at the Hall when there was mixed company, and when the conversation, therefore, was sure to be of a general nature. The priest, too, had not been invited since the affair of the chapel; her ladyship refusing to sit down to table with him, and alleging, as a justification of her conduct, the great insult which, through his instrumentality, had been done to her family and to her father's memory. Of course, her brother she did not consider so much to blame.

He was a tool in the hands of the priests, and seemed to think he could never humble himself enough for his past resistance to their authority. He was not very strong-minded at any time, and ill-health and pernicious advice had still further weakened his frame.

Except, then, upon the two or three occasions when there was company to dinner, the party consisted merely of Lady De Marbury, Sir John, Lord Clapham, and Mr. Marshall—a snug little quartet—and invariably, as a subject interesting, he knew, to each of the party, though for different reasons, Mr. Marshall would make a friendly attack upon his lordship on account of the religious opinions he had adopted. Mr. Marshall's arguments and reasons were all really of the most flimsy and transparent character, though clothed with a good deal of rhetoric and delivered with fluency and animation. He always proceeded on the assumption that his opinions were in accordance with the Bible, and that his opponent's were not so ; and, when reminded, as he would be, civilly by Lord Clapham that this was in reality only

begging the question, assuming the very point
that was a dispute between them, Mr. Marshall's
reply would consist merely of some vague reference
to his own feelings and conviction of the truth,
and such-like commonplaces.    With Lady De
Marbury all this declamation and confident assertion had great weight, and she wondered how any
one could resist her chaplain's eloquence; but to
Sir John, as to every masculine mind, the defects
in Mr. Marshall's logic were apparent enough.
He could see but little connection between most of
his premises and the conclusions he drew from
them, however he might try and mystify the
matter in a cloud of words and figures of speech.
He dealt in assertions when it was proofs that
were wanted, and declaimed instead of argued.
Lord Clapham had, therefore, but little difficulty
in dealing with such an opponent, and disposed of
him and his "arguments" with something like
contempt.

It must be allowed that the effect produced
upon Sir John's mind by these reiterated discussions was far from satisfactory, and that, instead

of building him up in the Protestant faith, which was the wish next to his mother's heart, his opinions were becoming more and more unsettled and indeterminate. Not that he had any serious thoughts of forsaking his own communion, especially during his mother's lifetime, but the idea was gaining ground in his mind, from what he had heard, that all the reasoning and arguments were on the one side, all the mere declamation and assertion on the other. He had been much struck with Mr. Marshall's own admission, when hard pressed by his noble opponent, that the " Protestant establishment," by which term he invariably designated the Church of England, "had the Apostles' doctrine, though not their fellowship;" an admission which his lordship made the most of, though Lady De Marbury was of opinion that the observation was a very striking and just one.

# CHAPTER VI.

It may be remembered that, at the commencement
of this history, it is related that Sir John and his
lawyer, Mr. Ardern, had had a long and serious
conversation, immediately after the former's coming
of age, upon the best steps to be adopted for relieving the estate of some of its embarrassments,
and that, amongst other measures devised, recourse
to an old man called Delves, residing in Newchurch, had been suggested, as a person able to
advance a considerable sum of money and at a
moderate rate of interest.    This project had not
been lost sight of, either by Sir John or his legal
adviser.    Indeed, the experience of a few months
only convinced them the more of the desirableness
and almost necessity of taking some such step, and

that before long. Though not extravagant in his habits, yet Sir John could but ill brook the idea of practising a rigid economy and foregoing those pursuits and amusements natural at his age, and to which his station seemed to entitle him; but many of these were such as involved considerable expense, and such as were little suited to the small income he had to live upon.

In country society the income of a person in Sir John's position soon comes to be pretty accurately known. Prudent mammas, with but slenderly portioned daughters, threw out their baits for others, but not for him. Ever welcome as a guest, and to be desired as a partner for a dance, yet he was not esteemed an eligible match for one of their daughters by those of his own rank and social position in the county. He was always spoken of as a "very poor man" by his own equals, and as one who could never think of marrying, unless it might be some one with a much larger fortune than any of the young ladies in that part of Cheshire could lay claim to. Marrying, however, and that at his early age, formed no part of

Sir John De Marbury's plans or aspirations; but he certainly did wish to hunt, and shoot, and fish, and to go into company, and to receive company, and to sport a handsome turn-out and ride a good horse, like the other Cheshire squires about him. But all this required money — implied a good income. It was not long, then, before Mr. Ardern's suggestions, by which some hundreds a year were to be added to his income, began to be seriously pondered upon; and steps at length were to be taken to carry them out. The most important of those suggestions had reference to a loan of £10,000, to be obtained from old Jacob Delves (as he was called by every one) by a mortgage upon the Donnington estates, and for which he was willing to accept the moderate rate of interest of four per cent. This Jacob Delves, at the time we speak of, was a little old shrunken man with whose shabby appearance about Newchurch two generations had been familiar. He had commenced life as a poor boy employed about the gardens of Donnington, in old Sir Thomas De Marbury's time. He had always had a great turn for saving, and used to collect nails and old pieces of iron, and gather scrapings on the road, to dispose of them in Newchurch. Afterwards he came to be employed as boots at the "Royal George" hotel in that town, where, after a few years, and by a life of great penuriousness, he contrived to save up a good bit of money. As he married a widow with some fortune of her own, his means became still further enlarged; and from this time, what between lending out small sums of money, at an enormous interest, to struggling little tradesmen, and what between a few fortunate mining speculations, he became richer and richer, until at last, in his old age, we find him in the proud position of being able to accommodate the owner of Donnington Hall with a loan of £10,000, and yet not to inconvenience himself thereby. Saving, saving, had been always his hobby from a youth; and probably the gratification of this sordid taste had been his only pleasure through life. He was quite a "character" in Newchurch; and people would stop to point him out as, with blear-eyed looks and seemingly bent half double, he would

grope along, as if searching in the kennel for
something he had lost.   He had never been known
to drink a glass of beer or any intoxicating liquor ;
nor had he ever given anything away in his life.
He was a privileged man ; nobody ever expected
him to give.   All the speculation was what he
would do with his money—to whom would he leave
it.   He had several poor relations in and about
Newchurch, but had long since, in order to avoid
their possible importunity, dropped their acquaintance and shut his door against them.   His house
was small and mean-looking, situated in one of the
back streets.   It had very little furniture in it,
and few visitors were ever known to cross its
threshold.   In this house the old man lived at the
time we are writing about, with a little girl, his
grand-daughter, as his only companion.   His wife
had been dead for some years, and the little girl,
now in her twelfth year, waited upon her grandfather and made him as comfortable as she could.
Her mother, who was a daughter of the old man,
and who had taken care of him for some time after
his wife's death, had, soon after the death of her

husband, married a second time, and gone to America and settled there. Little Annie Delves, as she was generally called, though her right name was Annie Eckersley, was a bright, good-tempered little thing, and kept the house and everything in it as tidily as possible. She had grown up under the eyes of the neighbours round about, and had received what little education she got at the neighbouring national school. After his way, the grandfather seemed to be fond of her, and to provide her with whatever she stood in need of. To all appearance, however, she was a poor person's child, and, in her dress, differed not at all from any of the neighbours' children about. So that, when Sir John De Marbury, in company with his solicitor, called upon old Jacob Delves, by appointment, to make final arrangements about the loan, and to seal and to sign certain deeds, he was astonished to see the old man's grand-daughter upon her knees, and busy scrubbing the passage. She got up upon recognising Mr. Ardern, and, with a courtesy to the strange gentleman, proceeded, her dress tucked up and her hands dripping from the pail, to throw open the parlour door. "Grandfather," she said, "here is Mr. Ardern and another gentleman wants to see you."

"Walk in, gentlemen, walk in," said the old man, coming to the parlour door and ushering them into a shabbily-furnished sitting-room where everything seemed much the worse for wear. There was a seemingly much-used old black horse-hair sofa, with two or three common painted deal chairs with rush bottoms, and a small rickety-looking mahogany table in the centre of the room. Including the carpet and some faded curtains, everything in the room would scarcely have fetched thirty shillings at a sale. The old man, nearly bent double, and wearing a green shade to protect his eyes from the sun, which happened to be shining in brightly at the time, received his visitors courteously and accommodated them with chairs. The business was soon entered upon; and a sort of scrivener, or irregular practitioner, whom Jacob employed about his affairs, having been summoned, and having, in conjunction with his employer, carefully examined the deeds and other papers connected with the transaction, finally the papers were all signed and sealed, as well as witnessed, and the greater part of them delivered over to the old man, who consigned them to his strong box. He then, his hands trembling with age, and his sight so impaired that he had to stoop over the paper to such an extent that his face almost touched it, wrote a cheque on a common piece of note-paper upon Messrs. Jones, Loyd, and Co., bankers, Manchester, for the sum of £10,000; and, with this precious piece of paper in his possession, Sir John De Marbury, as well as Mr. Ardern, wished the old man good-bye and took his leave, the granddaughter opening the door for them and courtesying and smiling pleasantly in acknowledgment of Mr. Ardern's notice as the visitors passed out. It was in this way that old Jacob Delves became the principal mortgagee upon the Donnington Hall estate. There were others, though for no great amount separately; and, as Mr. Ardern observed, it needed but another scratch of that old man's pen to wipe out the remaining claims. Sir John now returned in high spirits to the Hall, and for

some time afterwards gave full scope to his most
expensive tastes. He assumed for a time the
mastership of the Cheshire hounds, kept open house,
and served the office of high sheriff with brilliant
*éclat*, eclipsing all his predecessors (so he was told)
in the splendour of his liveries and general mag-
nificence of his turn-out. These things had to be
paid for in time, and Sir John soon found himself
again in straitened circumstances. His solicitor
shook his head when he talked about raising
money upon another mortgage, and intimated his
opinion that the thing could not be done. He
must retrench; he must get rid of those expensive
fox-hounds. There was nothing for it but to try
and live within his income. If everything else
failed, another application might be made by-and-
by to old Jacob Delves; but, for the present, and
coming so soon after the first loan, Mr. Ardern
would not recommend it. So Sir John was fain to
act upon this advice, and to accommodate himself
to his confined circumstances.

In the meantime the din of theological warfare
seemed rather to increase than to diminish at

Donnington. Sir John, it is true, took no part in it. He had many other things now to occupy his mind, which interested him much more. Besides, Mr. Marshall and his extreme opinions were more than ever distasteful to him. He had an undefined dislike to the man, and distrust in him, which he could not very well explain. And it was evident that, from some cause or other, the reverend gentleman did not stand quite so high in her ladyship's good graces as he used. So that, altogether, he was not such a frequent guest at the Hall as formerly; and, as the priest was still in Lady De Marbury's black books, it came to pass that the theological discussions which for a time occupied so large a share of the usual after-dinner conversation at the Hall almost entirely ceased. But what was gained in one way was lost in another. If the inmates of the Hall were left in peace, the storm raged all the more fiercely out of doors. Controversial lectures, two or three a week, were the order of the day. Mr. Marshall delivered a course of week-day lectures upon the distinctive doctrines and practices of the Roman Catholic Church, and denounced them so fiercely and wholesale that numbers came from all quarters to hear him. There would be occasional interruptions too—usually on the part of some excitable sons of Erin, who resented hearing the Pope spoken of as Antichrist—and so an "Irish row" not unfrequently added zest to the scene. As his "Roman Catholic brethren" were "affectionately invited" by Mr. Marshall to attend, these Patlanders used frequently to muster in full force, and to make their sweet voices heard to an extent that quite disconcerted the speaker. The success of these lectures was very far from answering the expectations of those who, like Lady De Murbury, encouraged Mr. Marshall— nothing loath himself certainly—to set them on foot. Results were indubitably produced, but not of the required kind. Inquiries were set on foot which were not so easily answered as the promoters of the lectures imagined. It is a law of human nature that persecution, or anything that wears that appearance, begets sympathy for the weaker party. And so, when people who had heretofore been indifferent enough to the merits of the controversy heard the Roman Catholic faith assailed in such bitter terms, and its ceremonies turned into ridicule, it led many of them to attend on Sundays at the little Roman Catholic chapel to hear what Father Delawney had to say upon his side of the question, and to judge for themselves whether the ceremonies practised there were quite as ridiculous as had been represented. This naturally led to interviews and explanations with the priest, and after a time to several "conversions." Few people amongst the middle and lower classes are in reality competent to form a judgment upon those subjects for themselves. They go by some rough rule of right and wrong which they have in their own minds. "The priest is such a *nice* civil-spoken man, and asked so kindly after mother," *therefore* "what he says cannot be wrong." "Things are not at all at the chapel as parson says. At least I saw none of it. They pray to God, and not to the Virgin Mary, the priest says. They only ask her intercession and prayers, as we might ask another to speak up for us. I see no harm in that anyhow; and the priest says he will be so glad to see any of us again if we have any more questions to ask him. He is a nice free-spoken gentleman, that he is, and I like him better any day than the t'other one who is so bigoted-like and uncharitable."

By some such process of reasoning numbers amongst the lower orders about Donnington, and even two or three of a rank somewhat above them, got into the way of attending the Roman Catholic services at Donnington. First it was occasionally, soon, in many instances, habitually, and then some would, after a while, renounce the Protestant faith and become Roman Catholics.

Lady De Marbury put down all these conversions to the unceasing activity and wiles of Father Delawney, and never dreamt of connecting them with her chaplain's lectures. She only saw in him a person who was apparently very diligent and active in counteracting the priest's proselytizing efforts, and readily accepted Mr. Marshall's oft-repeated assurance that things would

all come right by-and-by; that when the novelty
had worn off, and they had got tired of the
gewgaws of the Romish services (for which the
rector's innovations, he alleged, had given the
people a taste), they would come back soon enough
to the simple Scriptural services of his little church.
It was not until these conversions reached the
Hall itself that her ladyship was thoroughly
alarmed. But when, first, the under-housemaid,
and, subsequently, one of the grooms, requested to
be excused from attending Mr. Marshall's chapel
any more, and even showed some reluctance about
coming in to family prayers, upon the grounds of
their having become "Catholics" and having
been already received into "the Church" by
Father Delawney, the danger appeared too imminent to be regarded without serious apprehension. She could not help, therefore, testifying
some dissatisfaction to Mr. Marshall at the falling
away of so many of his flock, and treated with a
dryness of manner that was not usual to her his
allusions to the priest's wily snares and to the
semi-papistical services at the parish church.

Apparently Mr. Marshall thought it necessary,
after this expression of Lady De Marbury's dissatisfaction, to be up and doing something.   And
accordingly, when it was announced that *he* had
made a convert as well as the priest, his credit
began to rise again with her ladyship ; and, as
a boy was to be seen going about in his company
for a day or two, the news wore the appearance
of truth.   But, it coming out that the "conversion"
was from " Tractarianism," and not from Popery,
and that the subject of it—a discarded singing-
boy from the parish church—had made his submission to the rector (or rather his parents for
him) and had returned to his duties at Donnington
Church, Lady De Marbury's transient satisfaction
disappeared.   From the signs of the times it was
evident to all that a change at the Hall chapel
was impending, and that, when any decent pretext
presented itself, Mr. Marshall would be got rid of.
And so he seemed to think himself.   There was
an air of more independence about him, and he
seemed less desirous of conciliating Lady De
Marbury's esteem or good opinion.   He suddenly

abandoned, too, his lectures, and laid aside much of his controversial tone. Altogether, he seemed like one desirous of anticipating his dismissal by a "voluntary" resignation; and he was repeatedly and mysteriously absent, even to the disarrangement of his services, without thinking it necessary to assign any explanation or make an apology. But an event occurred which brought matters to a crisis sooner than might have been expected.

## CHAPTER VII.

Sir John De Marbury, as may have been
gathered, was a keen sportsman, and fond of
hunting in particular. When staying from home
for any time during the hunting season, he usually
took his horses with him, or rather sent them on
to be kept at some good stable in the neighbourhood where he was stopping. With the Warwick-
shire hounds in particular he was frequently in
the habit of hunting, especially when staying, as
he did commonly every year, for some weeks in the
early spring, at Leamington. Upon one occasion,
the meet happening to be at Aston, near Birmingham, Sir John sent his horses over the day before;
and, not being sure about the stable, and wishing
to look after his horses himself, he determined on

following them the same day, and sleeping in
Birmingham that night. He arrived at the " Hen
and Chickens" in that town in the course of the
afternoon ; and, having dined, and seen his horses
made up to his satisfaction, accident, and partly
fancy, took him in the direction of the Roman
Catholic cathedral—the only ecclesiastical edifice
worth looking at, he thought, in Birmingham.
It was about seven o'clock when he reached the
doors of the "cathedral," and from the rumbling
of the organ it was plain that a service of some
kind was going forward. So, pushing aside the
heavy curtain which was drawn across one of
the side doors, and groping through a dark
passage or two, he made his way into the body of
the church, which was filled with people, it being
the eve of one of the great days in the Romish
Church—the Feast of the Annunciation of the
B. V. M. Most of the people were on their knees,
gazing with uplifted eyes towards the splendidly-
decorated high altar, around which, from number-
less wax candles, shone a perfect blaze of light.
Flowers, both natural and artificial, decorated not

only the high altar and the side chapels, but also were twined round the pillars, and a wreath of lilies adorned the head of her who was the object of the coming festival, and whose image occupied a conspicuous place upon one side of the altar. Most of the people were kneeling, as we have said, and apparently engaged in adoring the figure we have described; others, who were on their knees also, were busily engaged in reading little books of devotion, only occasionally pausing to cross themselves, or to cast a look upon the services that were being performed at the altar; and others, again, like Sir John, were sitting somewhat in the background, and surveying the scene before them—possibly edified by it, possibly much the reverse. Sir John's feelings were probably something between the two : admiration of what he saw as a *spectacle*, and a sensation of shame, as if those whom he saw before him were so many pagan worshippers bowing down before yonder gaudily-attired image, holding a child in its arms, and with that tinsel crown upon its head. Notwithstanding the profusion of wax candles and oil lamps throughout the building, yet so dense were the clouds of incense floating about, and almost seeming to envelop the persons of the officiating priests, as they moved about the altar, sometimes dropping the knee to it, sometimes rapidly turning round and showing something to the people, which they would appear to hide and cover up immediately afterwards, and then to kneel down and pray to, that it was some time before Sir John could see very clearly what was passing, or understand at all what sort of service was being performed. From a neighbour, however, a looker-on like himself, he learnt that it was a " Benediction, with a sermon. The preacher was him in the black robe, of the Order of Jesus ;" and Sir John for the first time perceived a kneeling figure on one side of the altar, a little in front of it, and with his face sideways towards the congregation, but gazing—in a trance almost, it seemed, he was so wrapped up in the beatific vision—upon the Host, which was displayed on the altar. When Sir John's eyes first rested upon the kneeling figure he gave a start which attracted the notice

of those on either side of him, and then continued
to gaze with painful earnestness upon that kneeling form, never once withdrawing his eyes from
it.  At length, upon a signal from the organ,
which began to play a slow, solemn dirge, that
kneeling figure arose, and, slowly turning round,
displayed to Sir John's astounded eyes the features
of the *Rev. Paul Marshall.*  It was some time before Sir John could take his eyes off him, or pay
attention even to what he was saying.

"Who is that?" he asked of the same person he
had spoken to before, and indicating the preacher
by the direction of his eyes.

"Oh, that's the famous Father Paul, of whom
you may have heard.  He is a Jesuit, and is
coming back to this mission.  He has been
abroad, I believe, or somewhere."  And then the
speaker appeared to compose himself to listen with
attention to what such a famous preacher might
have to say.  Placing himself in such a way as to
interpose a pillar between himself and Father
Paul, Sir John listened with amazement to the
torrent of words which poured forth from his

lips, and in those accents which were so familiar
to him. Vituperation of Protestantism, and of the
English Church in particular, formed the staple of
his oration, as it might be called. At times he
would appear quite frantic with excitement, his
long black hair floating about him. At such
times a perfect stillness—as if there was a general
holding of people's breath—would prevail throughout the dense mass whom the preacher was addressing. He referred to his own bondage as an
English clergyman in times past, and, with a
fervour of thanksgiving almost amounting to
rapture, poured forth his thanks that the net
which had so long entangled him was broken, and
that he was set free. For upwards of an hour, it
might be said, did Father Paul hold that congregation absolutely entranced by his eloquence.
Sometimes he would lash himself into a perfect
storm of indignation, and his voice would echo
through and through the lofty building, as he
spoke of the daring, audacious enemies of Holy
Church, and their mad, impious designs against
her; and then, sinking his voice, would, in tones

of tenderest pathos that might have pierced the hardest heart, commend to the boundless mercy of the great Father in Heaven those unhappy, misguided beings who were lifting up their puny hands against the Vicar of Christ, and assailing with fruitless violence that Rock upon which His Church is built. It was not possible to be altogether proof against the charms of that fascinating manner; and it was only by summoning to his aid the recollection of the treachery and perfidy of which Mr. Marshall had been so long and undeniably guilty, that Sir John could bring himself to entertain a proper sense of indignation against him. To remain in Birmingham an hour longer than was necessary was, he felt, impossible; and so, hastily giving what directions were necessary to his groom, Sir John set off the same night by the mail-train, and, to the astonishment of his mother and of the whole household, arrived early on the following morning at Donnington Hall.

# CHAPTER VIII.

LADY DE MARBURY's indignation, of course, knew no bounds. Whatever else she had suspected, it could never have occurred to her that all Mr. Marshall's fierce denunciations against Popery were a mere sham, and that he was, in fact, and with a good deal of success, playing Father Delawney's game for him. Could the priest, she wondered, have been aware that the apparent Protestant minister was, in reality, a concealed Jesuit? There was nothing in Father Delawney's manner, or in anything he had ever said, to enable her to decide either way. His face always wore that smooth, oily, impenetrable look which may be said to be the badge of his tribe; he was never to be taken off his guard; and even now, though in her

ladyship's black-books, he treated her, when they
casually met in their walks, with the same un-
bounded deference and smiling civility that he
had ever shown during the three-and-twenty years
she had resided at Marbury. And, as for her
brother, the contemplation was a sad one! Who
does not know the degrading state of mental thral-
dom in which the Romish laity are held by their
priests? Where the interests of Holy Church are
in question, what will not its members say or do,
whether they be laics or ecclesiastics? And
then, in Lord Clapham's delicate state of health,
and with his morbid conviction of having been a
rebel of more than ordinary daring against the
authority of holy mother Church, what more
easy than so to work upon his feelings as to make
him look upon it in the light of a duty (in some
degree atoning for his former heresy) to aid and
abet Father Paul in his indefatigable efforts to win
back the De Marbury family, in the person of Sir
John, to the Catholic faith, and to help forward the
general work of conversion by such means as lay
in his power. Lady De Marbury did not know

what to think of her brother's share in the deception. For that he was aware of Father Paul's
real character before he left could not, she thought,
admit of any doubt. That secret midnight conversation, the suppressed laughter on the part of
Mr. Marshall which affected her so unpleasantly
at the time, though ignorant of its import, and
the slight air of confusion visible on her brother's
face next morning when he learnt that his sister
had, on that particular night, been the occupant of
the room adjoining his—all these things convinced
Lady De Marbury that her brother had, at any
rate, been put in possession of the secret before
quitting Donnington; but that he had advised
it, or even approved of it, seemed doubtful. That
an English gentleman, a peer of the realm, could
have abetted such a disgraceful imposition, she was
unwilling to believe, unless there was more evidence
to prove it than she was possessed of. Nay, those
two or three parting words of Mr. Marshall as he
left the room, that " everything was fair in war,"
would seem to imply—encouraged her, at any rate,
to hope—that Lord Clapham, priest-ridden as he

was, yet had sufficient of the feelings of an English
gentleman about him to condemn such an abuse of
his sister's confidence, and to have expressed his
disapproval of the plot.    She would cling to the
hope, at any rate.

It was on a Saturday morning that Sir John
returned.   He learnt, from inquiries immediately
instituted, that Mr. Marshall had been absent all
the week, and was not expected back until late
that same night.   Sir John's first impulse was to
write him a letter which he might get upon his
arrival, and to give orders for the immediate clos-
ing of the chapel, so that Mr. Marshall might not
again  desecrate  its  walls  by  his  ministrations
within them ; but there being some doubt—so
Mr. Ardern, at least, said—as to how far it would
be legal to close a duly licensed place of worship
without the bishop's authority (which there was
not time to appeal to, his lordship being in London), and Sir John being under the impression
that Mr. Marshall, as licensed minister of the
chapel (though it turned out afterwards, upon
inquiry, that he never had been actually licensed,

through some informality in his papers), could, and would probably, insist upon officiating until duly deprived by the bishop,—Sir John determined, being of a fearless, resolute nature, to attend the morning service as usual, and afterwards to confront the reverend gentleman and tax him with his deceit. In order the better to carry out his purpose, and to provide himself with an unexceptionable witness of what might pass between them, he wrote a note to his friend Captain Legh, of Ashton Hall, who happened to be at home on leave of absence, and requested him to be his guest at the Hall, and to aid him with his advice and presence in a matter of some emergency. The gallant dragoon promptly obeyed the summons, wondering much what was *up* now with Sir John. "Was he going to fight a duel?" This was his first question when he saw him; the next was—"Was it anything about poachers?" All the young man's thoughts, you see, running professionally upon "battle, murder, and sudden death."

But when he was told that it was only about a

parson, whom his friend wanted to get rid of, the young man's temporary excitement very speedily subsided. "Getting rid of a parson," so as he was not a rector or vicar, or with a great county following, seemed to him to be a very simple proceeding. It was looked upon quite in that light, in Cheshire, at the time I speak of, and is so still probably. If a curate, or friendless man, was so unlucky as to give offence to the squire, or to the squire's lady more probably, short work was made of him. The rector must at once get rid of him, if he valued the favour of the great people at the Hall, and did not wish all the parish charities to be thrown upon his hands; or the bishop would be written to—"Mr. So-and-so had made himself disagreeable;" or, perhaps, it was that he was making himself "*too* agreeable to one of the young ladies:"—it was requested that he might be removed, or else, &c., &c.; and so removed young Mr. Smith or Mr. Jones would be, with very little ceremony. So, when Captain Legh was told that his aid and presence were required to enable his friend Sir John to get rid of an obnoxious parson, he took the matter very quietly, only marvelling, as he stroked his moustache, in what way *his* humble services could be of use where it was only a parson that was to be demolished. After dinner, however, when the young men were left alone, and after the affair had been duly gone into, the young captain took more interest in the matter, and speculated even upon the part he might be called upon to play in the forthcoming *mélée*.

"By Jove! only to think of the fellow's assurance! He must have had a deuced deal of cleverness to play the game he has; only you must contrive to keep your temper with him, Jack. Those Jesuits, I imagine, are very difficult fellows to come over; and then you mustn't argue with him, my dear fellow, or he'll be sure to floor you. First tell him quietly that you are not going to stand any more of this sort of thing; and, if he gets at all impertinent, just leave him to me: I'll know how to manage him!"

Thus self-complacently did the young captain advise his friend as to what was to be his demeanour and course of proceeding for the next day.

Lady De Marbury did not think, of course, of attending the services of their own chapel on that Sunday. She hoped never to set eyes upon the wily Jesuit again, or to hear the sound of his voice. Great, then, was the sensation at the parish church when the little door opened which admitted into the family seat directly from the outside, and the tall, erect figure of Lady De Marbury was seen to enter, just a few minutes after the service had commenced. As she had not been at her parish church more than two or three times since the death of her husband, many were the speculations as to the cause of so unusual an event. The rector's wife, we may be sure, shared in the general surprise; and, as one object with her ladyship in coming over was to disburden her mind of its troubles to Mr. and Mrs. Hulton, they were not long left in doubt as to what had happened. The rector could not join her after church, being busy with his clothing club, or some such thing; but into the sympathizing ear of Mrs. Hulton, who, as she listened, was thinking all the time what a treat there was in store for her husband when he came

in to luncheon,—into her sympathizing ear did
Lady De Marbury pour the whole history of her
wrongs, and of Father Paul's deception; and, having
thus relieved herself, and being all anxiety to
learn what had passed between Sir John and Mr.
Marshall that morning, or perhaps what was
passing at that moment, she drove home.

"Well, I have something to tell you, Harry,
that will astonish you." It was thus that the
rector was greeted upon entering the house. "You
could never guess what has happened at the Hall."

"Something about Marshall, I suppose."

"Yes, something about him; but what do you
think it is?"

"He has been making up to the widow, perhaps.
All the single chaplains seem to go in for that."

"Oh, worse, worse—a great deal worse than
anything that has ever happened there before."

"Good gracious, Charlotte! what is it? Marshall
hasn't run off, has he? or he and the priest haven't
come to blows, have they?"

"Well, sit down and eat something while I tell
you. What do you think of this Mr. Marshall

being all the time a Romanist in disguise—an
actual Jesuit, Lady De Marbury says.   He is the
same Father Paul of the Oratory that there was
such a disturbance about two or three years ago.
You may recollect it : something about taking a
child away from its parents and concealing it ;—the
poor little thing died."

"I remember."

"Well, he is the very same Father Paul.   You
know he was a pervert.   He was one of the curates
of Brighton, and was run after so by all the evangelical young ladies ; when, all of a sudden, he went
to just the opposite extreme, and ended by going
over to Rome.   He went abroad, Lady De Marbury
said, and, when he came back, was only known as
Father Paul."

"He must have made use of his letters of orders,
and perhaps some old testimonials, to have imposed
upon the bishop.   I wonder the secretary didn't
twig him ; he is generally sharp enough—at least,
where money is concerned."

"Lady De Marbury says that Mr. Marshall once
told her something about his having a difficulty in

getting his papers signed, on account of his having been so long out of the country; but she never thought anything of it, of course."

"But how ever did it all come out?" asked the rector, hardly recovered from his amazement.

"Oh, Sir John happened to be over at Birmingham about something or other—he has been staying at Leamington, you know—and he went into the Romish cathedral out of curiosity, having nothing else to do; and one of the first persons he sees is Mr. Marshall (they call him Father Paul there); and Sir John heard him deliver *such* a sermon—so full of abuse against our Church; and then Sir John met some one in the train as he was coming back who was able to enlighten him a little more about Father Paul's antecedents."

"Well, I never heard such a thing before. You know I have often said to you that, if Marshall was paid for doing mischief to the Church, he couldn't have gone about it more effectually. The way in which he used to talk before Sir John was quite enough to unsettle any young man in his Church principles. Why, the priest used to beat

him out and out in his arguments, and not leave
him a leg to stand upon; and when I used to
uphold the catholicity of our Church and its
orders, why, this Marshall would be the first to
turn upon me and sneer at what I said, and represent that *his own*, and not mine, were the real
doctrines of the Church of England; and, of
course, he had plenty of authority quite at his
fingers' ends. It makes my blood boil to think of
it. However, I must be off: it is time for school."

We now turn to what was passing at Donnington Chapel at the very time the rector and his
wife were talking over Mr. Marshall and his
proceedings.

## CHAPTER IX.

As may be supposed, Sir John De Marbury's feelings were anything but comfortable as he and his friend took their seats in the great square pew in Donnington Chapel which belonged to the Hall. He had a great dislike to a *scene* under any circumstances. Especially he shrank from having openly hostile words with his clergyman—in his own church, too—and on a Sunday. But he was in a state of too much nervous irritation to brook delay: Mr. Marshall might leave directly after the services, or early on the following morning—might feign illness, or might give him the slip in some other way. Better, then, strike while the iron was hot. And there was something like a righteous retribution in exposing this man on the

I

very spot where he had so long carried on his
deceitful practices. Still he felt he should be very
glad when it was all over. While buried in such
thoughts, and looking with an air of abstraction
upon the congregation assembling by twos and
threes, mostly farmers and their wives, with a
sprinkling from Newchurch and one or two other
parishes—persons who considered it a privilege to
" sit under " Mr. Marshall, in preference to their
own respective clergymen,—while this was going
on, the little bell suddenly ceased its jingling, the
organ played out a voluntary, and in walked the
Rev. Mr. Marshall, looking calm and composed as
usual, and at once proceeded with the service.
There was one thing which seemed to strike him ;
and that was the empty pews generally occupied
by the Hall servants—a considerable array. None
of them were there. This, coupled with Lady De
Marbury's unusual absence, appeared to attract
Mr. Marshall's notice ; for his eye seemed to seek
Sir John's curiously on more than one occasion
during the service. The sermon, unlike any that
Sir John had ever heard from him before, was

short, delivered obviously without any preparation, and was rather a hasty commentary upon some portion of the services of the day than anything else. At length all was over, and the time had come for confronting the reverend dissembler. There was a good-sized vestry-room attached to Donnington Chapel, being intended also for the use of the Sunday-school, for Bible-classes, and the like; and in this room, which was furnished with a table, a few chairs and forms, it was Mr. Marshall's well-known custom to spend the couple of hours which intervened between the morning and afternoon services; so that Sir John made sure of finding him there when he should go in. Waiting, therefore, until all the congregation had dispersed, and the officials of the church were withdrawn, and the doors closed, Sir John then, accompanied by his friend, first knocked at the door of the vestry-room, and then entered it. They found Mr. Marshall in there, as they expected, and engaged with a book of devotion which looked like the Breviary, and which he made no attempt to conceal or put aside. Sir

John's face must have worn some peculiar expression, for the Jesuit seemed to read his purpose in
a moment. He stood up, and said in a steady,
fearless tone, " You have come, I suppose, to tell
me that you are aware who and what I am?"
Pausing for a moment, and gathering from Sir
John's expression that he was right in his surmise,
the priest went on. " Yes, you see before you no
pitiful Protestant minister of the Establishment,
but Father Paul of the Cross—an unworthy brother
of the Company of Jesus."

This was taking a high tone, and it somewhat
disconcerted Sir John in his intentions of delivering a sharp rebuke to him, and then leaving.

" Sir John De Marbury," said the priest, noticing
his momentary hesitation, " before you speak, before you utter words which you may repent of all
your life, listen to what I have to say. You
think, perhaps, in your blindness, that you come
here to degrade me—come here to tax me with
baseness. But I tell you that never was messenger of good news hailed with greater delight
than I welcome your presence here to-day. At

the bidding of the general of my order, and as some slight atonement for heresy long persisted in against the light, I have done *that* for well-nigh two years in comparison with which work at the galleys, labour fathoms deep in a mine, would have been embraced with transport. I have counterfeited the Protestant minister, have polluted my tongue with the language of heretics. But now joy! joy!" cried out the priest, his face radiant with delight, and in accents of thrilling emotion; "I have done with Protestantism and heresy for ever!—not in appearance even must I be for an hour longer what I so utterly loathe and abhor. *Laus Deo! Do tibi gratias, Domine.* 'The snare is broken, and we are delivered.'"

"Mr. Marshall, I come not here," said Sir John, with dignity, "to hear the faith of the Church of England reviled by an apostate—by one whose lips have been hitherto steeped in dissimulation. I come not even to 'degrade' you, as you have said: you have done that quite sufficiently for yourself. I shall not even stay to tax you with your inconceivable baseness and dissimulation——"

"Stop, Sir John," said the priest, with an air of authority; "you are not addressing some wretched culprit at Sessions. No, Sir John," and here the priest advanced a step or two, and, placing his hand on Sir John's arm, and looking steadily into his face, went on in a tone of mournful sadness; "you are heaping these taunts upon one who has been labouring night and day for your best happiness—endeavouring, if it might be, to win back to the faith the representative of the old Catholic family of the De Marburys. Oh, Sir John! refuse not my entreaty. I could kneel down to you if I could prevail on you to return to the bosom of that holy Church to which your forefathers belonged, of which all of that family whom you now represent were devout members. Talk not to me of degradation! of what avail men's idle notions about honour, compared with the saving of your soul? Oh, give me your conversion as my payment for all the pains and mortification I have endured on your account." The priest was too much in earnest to be repulsed with scorn. His eyes filled with tears, his voice shook, as he pleaded with pathetic earnestness, and besought the young man whose hand he grasped to make his submission to the Church at once, upon the very spot where they stood. Sir John was too much overcome to be able to reply at the moment. His friend, therefore, who had played a much less conspicuous part on the occasion than he expected, and whose presence in the room, indeed, the priest seemed hardly to have noticed, at length put in, and said—

"You don't expect, I suppose, that Sir John is going to forsake his religion? You will find yourself mistaken, by Jove! if you think so."

"Young man," said the priest, turning on him, and addressing him with authoritative voice, different from the tones of tenderness he had hitherto been using, "be content with killing human bodies: seek not to destroy souls as well. You are proud of your achievement in spearing ever so many of those wretched Sikhs in the war: lay aside such false pride; seek, with your friend here, admission, as a humble penitent, to the only one true Church. At any rate, stand not

now between your friend and the kingdom of
God."

Matters had turned out so completely different
from what they had expected, the priest had, all
through, assumed such a tone of superiority, that
the young men were only anxious now about
getting away.

"Mr. Marshall," said Sir John, gravely, "I
accept your assurance that what you have done
has been with a view to my benefit. You cannot
expect me, or any member of my family, to approve of the means which you have adopted to
effect your purpose. They are contrary, at any rate,
to the notions of honour with which I have been
brought up, idle as you may think them. But I
wish to part in peace with you. I have no intention of changing my religion, and must beg
not to be importuned further on the subject."

"Farewell, then," said the priest. "The seed
sown now may bear fruit hereafter. We shall
never meet more, Sir John, or, in all probability,
look on each other's faces again. I go, after a
brief stay at the oratory in Birmingham, first back

to Italy, to lay at the holy father's feet the results of my mission to England: they have not been altogether barren; and then, at the bidding of the general of my order, I shall have to cross many seas and traverse distant lands, even to the walls of China. There, as you know, the Catholic missionary carries his life in his hand from day to day. What shall befall me is known alone to Him whom I have faithfully endeavoured to serve. Farewell, then, Sir John De Marbury! Remember that the last words the Catholic priest ever addressed to you were to adjure you, by all your hopes of heaven, to seek for reconciliation with that holy mother Church whom you have so long slighted. And as for you, young man," went on the priest, turning towards Captain Legh, "you may tire yet of your inhuman trade of massacring your fellow-creatures, made, whether white or black, after the image of God, and of defacing His likeness by thrusting your cruel weapons into their bodies; remember that holy Church spreads out her arms for you as well as others, and invites you to take refuge within her everlasting gates!

and oh, remember, when struck down in battle, or
parched with fever in your hospital,—oh, remember,
at such times, if you have the power of thought,
my last words to you in this room. Fail not at
once to send, with the speed of lightning, for
some holy priest to receive your confession and
give you absolution before it be too late."

With these words the priest disappeared through
a side door, and was never seen again at Donnington.

Years afterwards though, when one of those
two young men who stood in the vestry-room of
Donnington Chapel on that particular Sunday
found himself under the walls of Canton, Father
Paul once more crossed his path. As aide-de-camp
to the general in command, Major Legh, as he
then was, had been more than once indebted for
local information and intelligence respecting the
movements of the enemy to a tea-merchant, who
spoke the language like a native, and dressed and
looked precisely like one. Major Legh had first
made his acquaintance in a joss-house, which he
had gone to see, with some of his brother officers,

out of curiosity, and where the seeming merchant was engaged assisting at some native ceremony. This man appeared to attach himself to Major Legh almost from the first, and had given him to understand that he was in reality a Christian missionary. He was missed after a time, and nothing heard of him until nearly the termination of the war, when one night, late, a person disguised as a Malay sailor, but who was indeed a French priest, conveyed a token from the seeming tea-merchant which left no doubt of his identity. It was a scrap of paper, on which these words were written : " Father Paul of the Cross. Remember Donnington Chapel, Sunday, April —, 184—."

"That piece of paper was given me by Father Paul," the French priest went on to say ; " and he charged me, as a dying request, to place it myself in your hands if I ever escaped from the prison in which we were both confined. Father Paul was led out to execution shortly afterwards, and, by the express order of Commissioner Yeh, and under his personal superintendance, was sawn asunder."

Such was the fate of Father Paul, as it became known long afterwards. The French priest, it seems, contrived to escape in the disguise in which Major Legh saw him.

## CHAPTER X.

Lady De Marbury was, of course, all eagerness for the return of her son and his friend from church. She had to wait a long time, however, before her curiosity as to what had passed between them and the disguised Jesuit was gratified. At length, as she stood watching at one of the Hall windows, she saw Sir John and Captain Legh walking slowly towards the house. There was an air of reserve and thoughtfulness, and an indisposition to enlarge much upon what had so recently passed at the chapel, that struck her with surprise as they entered. She was prepared for a graphic, perhaps amusing, account of a " scene " with Father Paul, and for the display of a good deal of excitement on the part of both the young men ; but, instead of that, she merely learnt from her son that Father Paul had at once admitted the deception he had so long practised, and had alleged that his motives were good for acting in the way he had done.

"His motives!" exclaimed Lady De Marbury, indignantly; "what might *they* have been, pray?"

"He wished me to conform to the Catholic Church," her son replied, rather sadly, and taking up a book.

"Wished you to become a Papist! I hope, John, you gave him a good talking to when he dared to speak to you in that way, and to try and brazen the thing out?"

"I didn't say much to him. I only said I had no intention at present of changing my religion."

"At present! then do you mean to say you held out any prospect to him that such a thing was possible?"

"Well, I forget the exact words I used," replied Sir John, apparently anxious to drop the subject. "I only know I said that I was not going to become a Romanist."

" Why, my dear John, you talk as if this man had some control over you—as if *you* were the person who had reason to dread his displeasure! I hope you told him pretty plainly what we all thought of him ?"

" Why, you see, his intentions were, no doubt, good."

" Well, I have no patience with you, I declare! to allow yourself to have been talked over by this wily Jesuit in the way you have been, and after the shameful manner in which he has acted towards your mother and everybody else! What do *you* say, Captain Legh ?—*you* were not afraid of him, I suppose ?"

" Why, you see, Lady De Marbury," said the captain, sitting down to luncheon and evading the question, "he is a deuced clever sort of fellow, and all that."

" Stuff and nonsense!" said her ladyship, with rising displeasure. " Good intentions, cleverness; what next will you both say in his favour? I am really ashamed of you both, that you should have let this wily, scheming Jesuit off so easily. If it hadn't been Sunday, and if I had thought that he would have made such fools of you both, why, I would have sent the two footmen down to give him a good ducking in the mere."

"It is better as it is.   He says he is going to China shortly."

"To play the same game with the Chinese! He may meet his match there, if he is caught at it."

"It is extraordinary," said Captain Legh, with an absent manner, and addressing no one in particular, "what these men will not undergo in order to spread their faith.   There is really a kind of sublimity about their self-devotion, in the sacrifices they are ready to make, that one cannot help admiring."

Apparently this remark was as little to Lady De Marbury's taste as anything that had fallen from either of the young men since they came in; for, pushing back her chair, she quitted the table with some abruptness, and was not visible again until dinner-time, when all traces of displeasure had disappeared from her usually placid features, and the name of Father Paul seemed to be avoided by general consent.

It had been agreed in the morning that Mr. and Mrs. Hulton were to come over to luncheon next day; and Lady De Marbury had the satisfaction of knowing that, in the rector and his wife, she would have warm abettors, and that nothing she could say against Father Paul would be too bad in their estimation. Accordingly, at luncheon-time next day they arrived, and very soon Father Paul and his delinquencies formed the subject of conversation. Captain Legh had left, and Sir John was out about the place somewhere; so Lady De Marbury had it all her own way for some time at least.

"Would you believe it, Mr. Hulton, that Sir John and Rowland Legh were actually half defending Mr. Marshall yesterday — were talking about his good intentions, and his cleverness, and all that stuff—not a word about his treachery and shameful behaviour?"

"I hope to goodness he can be well punished: one would have no patience with his getting off."

K

So spoke Mrs. Hulton, looking very pretty and animated all the time, as she advocated what she called " decided measures " against the Jesuit.

" Well, I have no love for the man myself," said Mr. Hulton; " but I believe the best thing would be to let him go quietly out of the country —if to China, all the better; and I only wish he would take that wily priest Delawney along with him."

" Wouldn't it be most desirable, Mr. Hulton, if we could break up the nest of them here, and get rid of the priest and chapel and all? You know it has been tried once or twice. I mean to speak to Sir John about it. But here he comes himself."

" I have been down," said Sir John, after he had greeted his visitors and joined the party at luncheon, " as far as Mr. Delawney's. I wanted to ask him what he knew exactly about this business of Marshall's."

" Well, did you see him? and what did he say?" inquired Lady De Marbury anxiously.

" He said that latterly he had his suspicions."

" But did you ask him the question point-blank," said the rector, "whether he knew that Mr. Marshall was a disguised Jesuit when he used to come here and carry on those discussions with himself?"

"I understood him to say he was ignorant of it at the time. At least, he implied as much."

"You didn't get much out of him, John, it seems."

"Not much."

"We were saying just now, before you came in," said Mr. Hulton, after a pause in the conversation, "that it would be well if you were to try and get rid of the whole concern, priest and chapel and all, out of Donnington : buy them out, if necessary : it would contribute very much to the peace of the parish."

"The same idea has occurred to myself, and I intend to speak to Mr. Ardern about it. I should think a place of worship and a residence in New-church, where the bulk of his congregation are, would be much more convenient to the priest. But I shouldn't be for doing anything hastily : it might hurt his feelings."

"Hurt his feelings!" exclaimed Lady De Marbury, turning up her eyes to the ceiling—a favourite mode of hers when she would intimate dissent without expressing it in words.

"You are too good-natured, Sir John," put in pretty little Mrs. Hulton, whose satisfaction would have been complete if the priest could have been severely punished as well as Mr. Marshall.

"He is quite as deep as the other," said Mr. Hulton, "and I would stand on no ceremony with him. I would get rid of them root and branch out of the place, if I were you."

"Well, we'll see what is to be done. And now about the duty at our chapel: what arrangement is to be made? I don't intend to have any more chaplains resident here. They have been altogether a sad nuisance."

"I think you had better let me provide for the duty. I can send one of my curates, and you can give me £50 a year, and that will help to make out his salary. There isn't enough here to occupy a man's time, and so they take to pernicious or foolish courses."

The last words came out rather awkwardly, and
the rector tried to check himself. His hesitation,
however, attracted Lady De Marbury's attention,
and her thoughts rambled off for a moment from
Mr. Marshall to poor MacMahon, with his "Oirish
melodies" and "poethrey" nonsense. The same
thought probably occurred to Mrs. Hulton, for she
straightway fell to admiring some flowers upon
the table, and to questioning Sir John about his
conservatory.

So the thing was settled in a few words, that
Mr. Hulton was in future to provide for the duty
at Donnington Chapel by himself or curates; and
thus that which had been formerly such a bone of
contention between the Hall and the Rectory was
quite quietly disposed of, and without a word of
objection on the part of Lady De Marbury. It
is true that her reign at the Hall was over, and
that the power had passed into other hands. She
was also talking of taking a house at Bath, and
going to reside there; so that her interest in
Donnington Chapel, and in the selection of a
minister for it, had naturally much diminished;

and so she acquiesced in the rector's arrangement
as the best that could be made under the circumstances.

"I shall one of these days," said Sir John,
"whenever I am rich enough, be for pulling down
that chapel, and building a handsome church with
a spire in its stead. It would look very well
through the trees; and perhaps we might have a
district assigned to it."

"Come," thought Lady De Marbury to herself,
"it is not so bad, after all. He talks of building
a church and getting rid of those Jesuits. He
can't be thinking of turning Papist, after all."

## CHAPTER XI.

THERE was a positive calm in the moral atmosphere after the departure of Mr. Marshall; and as for conversions, such things speedily ceased to be talked about, or to occur. By degrees, most of those who had got into the way of attending the services at Father Delawney's little chapel slunk back into their places at church, and seemed heartily ashamed of their temporary perversion. Even the contumacious groom had, after the departure of his Susan (upon the expiration of her month's warning), expressed such an invincible dislike to fasting and going to confession, that no difficulty at all was found in inducing him to resume his attendance at church. Being a young man of somewhat fickle disposition, it was

not long before he and Susan's successor in the
brush and dustpan department were "keeping
company" with each other, and visiting on the
sly, when it was her "Sunday out," a little white-
washed meeting-house on the outskirts of the
parish, whither the disaffected in church matters
were wont to resort. Altogether, things returned
very much to the *status in quo*, and soon Mr.
Marshall and his plot had gone the way of other
nine-days' wonders.

Shortly after the above occurrences, Lady De
Marbury had carried out her long-talked-of plan
of taking a house at Bath and going to live there.
There was at that time a famous preacher—a
countryman of Mr. MacMahon's, by the way—at
the Octagon Chapel in that city; and this circumstance had, no doubt, very much turned the scale
in favour of Bath.

Lady De Marbury's departure from the Hall
was viewed with a good deal of secret satisfaction
by most of the county magnates, with whom she
had never been very popular. Sir John, it was
thought, would come out more now, and throw

his house open to the county. Donnington Hall
had been under an eclipse too long, and its restoration into the cycle of " entertaining houses " would
be hailed with universal satisfaction. The only
thing wanting was to find a suitable wife for Sir
John. She must have money, that was certain;
and if she was Cheshire born and related to any of
the " ruling families," why, so much the better.
The young lady who was principally talked of for
him, and who answered most of the necessary requirements to be sought for in the future mistress
of Donnington—though, unfortunately, not the
principal one—was Mrs. Hulton's sister, Miss
Townley. As she was often staying at the Rectory, and as she went about everywhere in that
part of the county, it necessarily happened that
she and Sir John were brought into frequent con-
tact, and were, indeed, upon intimate terms. This
young lady had beauty, and was possessed of all
her sister's lively, agreeable manners, and was considered to be fully as accomplished; but, unluckily,
her fortune was not large—a simple five thousand
pounds; and here was the difficulty. For that she

and Sir John liked each other well enough was no
mystery in county circles, only it seemed clear
that they were not rich enough to marry—at any
rate, during Lady De Marbury's lifetime, her considerable jointure constituting a serious burden
upon the estate ; and Lady De Marbury's life was
good for many years to come.

Mrs. Hulton did, indeed, try her hand at making
up a match between her sister and Sir John, and
would sometimes talk the matter over with her
grave husband, who was some years older than
herself.    Time was, indeed, when Mr. Hulton
himself was no despicable match in the eyes of
match-making mammas.    He had the three
requisites which Cheshire magnates look for in
aspirants to their daughters' hands : he had
Family, Fortune, and was Presentable.    Other
things are very well in their way—amiability,
talent, morality, and so on ; but let a man have
these three qualifications, and he will be acceptable
anywhere in the county, unless there be something
*very* outrageous indeed in his goings-on.    And
Mr. Hulton, then the life and soul of gaiety, fully

came up to the mark; and it was not long before
his capture was effected, and he was led about in
triumph by her who now sat so contentedly by his
side, and who went hand-in-hand with him in all
his plans for the good of the parish, and who
worked as assiduously at her school, and read to
the old people, and physicked the ailing, as if she
had never been the belle of the Newchurch assemblies and the glory of many a Cheshire ball-
room. Her great wish now was to bring about a
match between her sister and the squire. Why
shouldn't they be able to live upon £800 a year?
Mightn't some uncles or aunts die and leave them
money? If anything were to happen to Lord
Clapham, and to that sister of his who was so
delicate, would not a good deal of the property come
necessarily to Sir John? She was quite certain
that *something* would turn up. And then it would
be such a nice thing to have Lotty at the Hall,
instead of that disagreeable old Puritan the
dowager. It was quite worth while, at any rate,
to make an effort to bring the thing about.

Mr. Hulton, as has been intimated, was once himself the subject of a somewhat similar speculation, upon the part, not of her who was now his loving wife, but of her mother (she had been a Miss Parker). *His* fortune had been well looked into ; *his* tastes and habits quietly scanned ; and, when it was decided that he was worth catching—the line had been thrown out by skilful hands—the bait, after a little trifling with it, was taken, and the prize landed. All this was past and gone— forgotten almost—as if it had happened a hundred years ago. Mr. Hulton was only too happy in his captivity, too proud of his chains, to care to inquire too minutely into the process by which his capture had been effected. And now, when his little wife talked over with him the best way of bringing about a match between her sister and the squire, no tame elephant conducting his fellows into a trap could have been more amenable than was the rector to do her bidding. Yes, he thought it *would* be a very nice thing to see Lotty at the Hall. He was quite willing to aid the project. Let them have Lotty on a visit, and then ask Sir John to dine every now and then.

He was alone, too, at the Hall, and would be glad
of some lively girl to chat with. Only point out in
what way he (the rector) could be serviceable, and
he would be only too happy. Might he now go out
into his parish? he had several sick people to visit.
And thus the matter was settled for the present.
But it is one thing to make arrangements for two
other people—that they should marry; that it is
the very thing for them—and quite another for
the parties themselves to fall in with your plans,
either one or both. Lotty was capricious. Lotty
*would* flirt with young Davenport—she seemed to
prefer him to the baronet; she would get to cross-
purposes with her sister, and contrive to mar her
little projects in the most provoking way possible.
Perhaps it was that she thought Sir John was
dilatory in coming to the point—that they had
been talked of too much as it was, if nothing was
to come of it.

Perhaps it was; but who can penetrate into
the recesses of the female heart, and follow all
its windings? Lotty's tactics may have been
the best, after all. Was she not her mother's

daughter ? as if that was not quite enough.   You
and I, common-place persons as we are, might
have blundered out our meaning.    That little girl,
though not quite eighteen, would have been more
than a match, I suspect, for us both.  Sir John
seemed rather disconcerted by the young lady's
waywardness.    Some barrier seemed to have
arisen between them.    Was it that Mrs. Townley
(whose fame as a match-maker was spread over
Cheshire) had been giving her daughter a hint ?
There was no finding her alone, or getting to sit
next to her at dinner.   She was "at home" at
the Rectory, and could contrive to sit pretty
much wherever she had a mind.   Why should
she encourage that young Davenport to be always
dangling after her, and coming over so often from
Malpas ?  Sir John's case was one that required
very careful handling.   Perhaps Lotty had *hardly*
experience enough to deal with it.   It was a case
for her mother.  *She* would no doubt have displayed her usual acumen.   For you see it was
this way : Sir John's was not *simply* a case of
holding back : there was no indisposition on his

part to make Miss Lotty an offer—*that* came out afterwards, only it was too late; but the young man knew his own circumstances best—knew that he had difficulty enough as it was to make both ends meet; how would it be, then, with a gay fashionable girl like Charlotte Townley as his wife? How could he ever hope to satisfy Mrs. Townley's requirements (there was a Mr. Townley, but no one ever thought of *him* in these matters) as to jointure and pin-money, and all those con-comitants to matrimony? She might give him credit for being better off than he was. How mortifying to be obliged to disclose the real state of his finances, that he had barely £700 a year to live upon, and with an expensive place like the Hall to keep up! If Sir John had had an oppor-tunity of unfolding the matter to that experienced lady Mrs. Townley, it is probable that things might have turned out differently from what they did. But, discouraged as he was by the way in which Miss Lotty met his advances (it is possible she saw her error afterwards), and distrusting his acceptableness with the family on account of his straitened means, it is certain that Sir John made no sign during Lotty's somewhat protracted stay at the Rectory; and so Mrs. Hulton's little plan for making the two young people happy came to nothing.

# CHAPTER XII.

LITTLE is ever heard in Newchurch of old Jacob
Delves: on fine days he just gets outside his door
and basks in the sun. It can never be too warm
for the old man. The cold creeps into his marrow,
and it is with difficulty that the vital heat is sustained in him. The doctor tells him to live well,
to take nourishing things, to drink a little wine
—that a glass of gin-and-water, the last thing at
night, would do him no harm. But Jacob has
been too long accustomed to his old penurious
ways to begin indulging himself now. He dreads
being reduced to want. The only pleasure of his
life has been to hoard up money. Deprive him of
that, and you deprive him of the only object worth
living for, in his estimation. His sight is too weak

to permit him to read much. Little Annie, his grand-daughter, reads him a chapter in the Bible every now and then. He likes to hear her read, and to notice her improvement. The long words and proper names are no longer slurred over, and a chapter in the Old Testament is not the formidable thing to her that it was a short time back. It is difficult to say what sense the old man puts upon many of the parts read to him which enjoin liberality, bountifulness, and the like. It is certain that he never acts upon them. He has never been known to give a subscription towards any object in his life, and, were it not for little smiling Annie, who puts by the scraps, and has always something to give away, many a beggar would have turned from his door with bitterness in his heart and curses on his lips. Old Jacob's nearest relations, two sisters and their children, pass and re-pass the old man as he sits sunning himself at his door; but greeting for them he has none. Their inquiries after his health elicit no kindly response; in fact, he does not like to see them about him; and as for that tall, hulking young fellow, his nephew, who never seems to have anything to do but to worry him with questions, and to interrupt little Annie at her work, he cannot endure the sight of him. Perhaps the young man considers himself as his heir, and this may account for his never having done anything for himself. He lives with his mother, and depends upon her hardly-earned money, as a laundress, to supply himself with beer and tobacco and other indulgences; or it may be, when he loiters so long about his uncle's door, and watches for Annie as she goes for the milk or trips out upon any little errand for her grandfather, that the young man would establish for himself an interest in that little damsel's heart. "The old fellow may leave his money to *her*, after all, and not to me: who knows?" It is a problem that he is perpetually engaged in solving, "To whom will the old man leave his money?" and though viewed in ever so many different lights, amidst clouds of tobacco, and under the peculiar sort of inspiration produced by more than one glass of spirits-and-water, quite irradiating the young man's imagination and filling him with golden

visions of the future, yet it must be admitted
that he is no nearer a solution at the end of his
cogitations than he was before.

It was certain that the old man had the money—
as much as £30,000, it was said : wouldn't *he* know
how to spend it ?—and it was certain that this
money must come to somebody, or be divided.
But further than this Tom Swigmore had never
been able to get.  Surely the old man wouldn't
be such an unnatural wretch as to leave all his
money to an hospital, to an infirmary, to the parsons to build churches with!  The thought was an
agonizing one, and at a certain period of the young
man's potations would bring tears to his eyes.
But others, besides Tom Swigmore and the family,
had an eye upon old Jacob, and would speculate
as to what he would do with his money.  No one
thought he would part with any of it in his
lifetime.  But then he was upwards of eighty,
and could not go on living for ever.  It was doubtful whether any of his relations would receive
much of his money : perhaps a few hundreds might
come to Annie ; that was all, it was thought.

From his character and peculiarities it was more likely that old Jacob would leave the greater part of his money to some public institution—to the Queen, it was even suggested; and so there would be no harm in putting before him the claims of a few of the most deserving of the public charities and of the religious societies, in case old Jacob should be at any loss what to do with his money. Accordingly, every now and then the post would bring him a case of "Alarming Spiritual Destitution in the Potteries," or an "Appeal in behalf of the Manchester Infirmary," or a paper headed "Hasten to the Rescue," and setting forth the claims of some ragged school, or Magdalen asylum, or juvenile reformatory, or what not; and not unfrequently it would be an urgent representation of the imperative duty on the part of Englishmen of sending out missionaries to Patagonia or Timbuctoo, or even despatching them into Ireland to convert the natives there.

Jacob did not seem to dislike getting these papers; and so, instead of throwing them into a waste-paper basket (supposing he possessed such a thing), he would con over one of these for days together, apparently trying to master some fact or statistics in them, and then, when he had quite done with it, or its place had been supplied by another, he would carefully tie it up and add it to a heap of similar papers, which he kept on one of the shelves of his sitting-room. It may be he had some idea of responding to the appeal ; there may have seemed to him some merit even in the entertaining of such a bountiful thought; or perhaps it was merely the result of his old habit of hoarding : they would fetch something as waste-paper. Like most of his class, who have risen from nothing, and who have been scraping money together all their days, old Jacob was fond of dilating upon his early struggles. He would dwell upon his having been originally a poor boy employed about the gardens of Donnington Hall, glad to earn a penny in any honest way; often obliged to dine off a hard crust; thankful for any scraps the cook had no use for. He would dwell upon the glories of Donnington in those days, and describe some of Sir Thomas's feats in the hunting-field, and recall with pride

his chance notice of himself, and tell how Sir
Hugh, in after-days, wished him to be his coach-
man, but that he was doing better for himself as
head hostler of the "Royal George;" and so the old
man would ramble on about his early days, with
little Annie usually as his listener. She knew the
whole history of the De Marburys, from Sir
Thomas's father downwards, so repeatedly did
they form the subject of the old man's talk. She
knew all about their marriages, and christenings,
and funerals, and how the ladies dressed themselves in old times. It was the one subject that
interested her grandfather, and she was content to
listen to his oft-told tales with that exemplary air
of interest that all her sex know so well how to
assume. She gave promise of being pretty, did
Annie, had fine dark eyes, fair hair, pure transparent complexion, and a bright, pleasant expression of countenance. She would talk upon those
subjects the old man liked to dwell upon, and had
at all times a loving, gentle manner with her
towards him which won upon him more and more,
so that he could scarcely bear her out of his sight.

"Ah," he would often say to her, stroking her head fondly, "if I could only see my little Annie a lady, *that* would make your old grandfather happy! You are not fit to rough it: these little dainty hands were never meant for the scrubbing-brush. Why shouldn't you hold up your head with the best of them? I have money enough, if that is all." And then the old man would keep on muttering something to himself. He seemed to be breaking fast, and often now complained of restless nights. He had been a hale, hearty man in his time, had old Jacob, even when getting perceptibly into years. Down to comparatively a recent period he had been engaged in the Stafford-shire pottery trade and in coal-mine speculations, by which he had amassed a large fortune. During all that time, and while a resident in the Potteries (Sir Richard then reigned at the Hall), Donnington affairs were a blank to him; he knew of little that was passing there, and nothing scarcely of Sir Richard himself; and, since his return to New-church, and during the long minority of Sir John, there was nothing stirring at the Hall of a nature to engage his attention. Sir John's visit to him, however, with Mr. Ardern, had revived his interest in the family, and the old man seemed to recur to it with gratification. He dwelt upon Sir John's good looks and free and pleasant manners, and heard with interest any little details connected with his habits and pursuits. Things were in this state, and the old man was in the house, and complaining of being poorly, when a visitor made his appearance in the person of Mr. Ardern. His business was soon explained : Sir John was likely to be put to inconvenience by the calling in of a considerable sum of money which had been advanced to the late Sir Richard to enable him to complete the purchase of some land, and which had remained a charge upon the property ever since. Could Mr. Delves lend the money, and at the same rate of interest that the former loan had been had of him ? The money required was £5000. Old Jacob took some time to answer. He then said—

" If I were to lend this money, Sir John would be in my debt £15,000—a large sum. I must

think the matter well over. Has Sir John any
means of repaying the whole sum if I require it
for any purpose, and after reasonable notice?"
And the old man fixed his still keen eyes upon the
lawyer and awaited his answer.

"Well, only by going into the market. I suppose he could still raise enough off his property to
pay you in full, though it might put him to some
temporary inconvenience."

"Well, Mr. Ardern, I'll think over it; and, in
the meantime, will you ask Sir John to call upon
me? I should like to speak to him before making
any promise."

After this conversation, and upon the departure
of the lawyer, the old man seemed buried in reflection. He spoke little, but remained sitting
over the fire.

"Business with these lawyers is more, grandfather, than you are well able for, now. You had
better leave it to Mr. Dean." This was the name
of the scrivener, or actuary, who managed most of
Mr. Delves's affairs for him.

"It is so cold," said the old man, spreading his

shrivelled hands before the fire. "But I shall be better when I have had my tea."

As he had been complaining of not feeling well for two or three days, Annie felt more alarm than she otherwise would. She had not been in the room when Mr. Ardern called, but, taking it for granted that it was upon business, and business, perhaps, of an exciting nature, she had made the suggestion of sending for Mr. Dean, and leaving him to settle the business with Mr. Ardern. Nothing more was said upon the subject. But the old man still complaining of cold and shiverings, Annie stepped out and despatched a messenger for Mr. Wright, old Jacob's usual medical attendant.

"He has got a touch of this influenza that is going about," pronounced Mr. Wright, after feeling his pulse and examining his tongue. "You had better go to bed early, Mr. Delves, and I'll send you some medicine."

"Is grandfather very bad?" asked poor little Annie, putting the corner of her apron to her eyes.

" No; it is nothing but a cold he has caught. Still, eighty-three—I think that is his age, is it not ?—eighty-three is a disease in itself."

The old man did not rest very well that night, and when he awoke there was an increase of feverish symptoms about him. He expressed a great desire to see Sir John De Marbury, and, accordingly, a message to that effect was soon despatched to Donnington Hall. " Sir John was out riding," the messenger brought back word, " but as soon as ever he came in he should be told of Jacob's wish to see him." As the day wore on the feverish symptoms somewhat abated, leaving, however, the old man very weak. It was just getting dusk when the sound of horses' feet under the window aroused the patient from a brief slumber, and directly afterwards the old woman who was nursing him announced " Sir John De Marbury."

" Let every one leave the room," said the old man feebly, looking towards the nurse and two or three who had upon some pretence come into the room. " I wish to speak to Sir John De Marbury quite alone ; and let the door be shut." These directions being obeyed, Sir John, seating himself at the bed-side, prepared to listen to what the sick man might have to say to him.

# CHAPTER XIII.

THE last rays of the sun faintly lighted up the sick
chamber.   There were the usual tokens of illness
about the room: half-emptied bottles; an orange or
two; the tea-cup, with a spoon in it, out of which
the last nauseous powder had been taken; and then
the sick man's clothes which he had for daily use,
stowed away here and there, as if not likely to be
wanted soon again.   Who has not before his eyes
some such chamber, with its windows slightly open
at times for purposes of ventilation?   The furniture in Jacob's sleeping-room, like that down-stairs,
was old, and of a heterogeneous description, as if
picked up at a sale or broker's.   But the bed-linen
and all belonging to it, as well as the curtains, were
perfectly neat and clean, and altogether the old

man wanted for nothing. He lay there on the bed, breathing with some difficulty, but free from actual pain, only very weak, he said. Sickness such as his is a great leveller of distinctions, and so Jacob Delves took little notice of Sir John De Marbury as he entered the room and sat down by the bedside, and only gave the direction already mentioned, speaking in feeble and husky tones, that all else should leave the room. After a little pause the old man began, speaking at first in a very low tone, but his voice gaining strength as he proceeded:—

"I feel, Sir John, as if I was not likely to be here very long, and there is something on my mind I have to say to you which concerns us both. I am an old man, in my eighty-third year, and have worked hard in my time for my living. I began life, as you know, at the Hall, and I wish, when I am dead and gone, that my bones should rest in Donnington Churchyard, under the old elm-tree which I have so often climbed as a boy: will you promise me that—that you will see it done?"

A squeeze of the hand assured the dying man of Sir John's readiness to see his wish complied with.   He then went on :—

"I have always loved Donnington and everything belonging to it.  I was poor there, and happy, before the cares of riches and of money-making took such hold upon me.  Now it is about this money I want to speak to you.  When Mr. Ardern told me, two years ago, that he thought you would be glad to borrow of me, I was proud to accommodate the owner of Donnington, and let you have the money on easier terms than were customary with me.  Since then—it was only yesterday, though it seems longer—Mr. Ardern has been to me again, to say that you wished to borrow £5000 more, which would make in all, if I were to lend it to you, £15,000.  Now, Sir John, I can't do this in the way you wish.  I am going out of the world—the doctor says I can't last more than a few days—and I wish to settle my affairs at once. I have no one except my little grand-daughter, whom you may have seen, whom I care for, or who cares for me.  It is only my money they want.  I have provided, therefore, for Annie, so that she shall never want, and left a few hundreds amongst my sisters and their children. But the bulk of my property, amounting in all to £20,000, goes to the Manchester Infirmary, and to one or two other institutions. They will be sure to call in at once the £10,000 I lent you; and Mr. Ardern tells me that this may put you to much inconvenience. If I was to lend you another £5000, your difficulties would be all the greater."

Here the old man paused for breath, and being supplied, at his request, with a mixture of some sort, seemed to feel a little recruited. He then, with great difficulty, raising himself up in bed, took from under his pillow a paper, and then went on :—

"This paper is my will, by which my directions will be carried out as I have just described them to you. It has been fairly written out, and is ready for execution this evening—in half an hour hence. It only wants my signature and those of witnesses to be binding. Once I am passed away, and you will be in the hands of the Governors of the Manchester

Infirmary, and such as them; and you know what sort of creditors *they* are likely to prove, and how little they'd care if they were to ruin all the De Marburys in the world. You understand me?"

"Perfectly," said the young man.

"Now, Sir John," and here the old man's voice quivered, "I have not sent for you merely to tell you this—for you would know it quite soon enough—but I have sent to tell you that it rests with yourself, and yourself alone, whether I carry out my purpose of leaving all my money to public institutions, or whether, with the trifling exception of a few hundreds, all my money goes to *yourself.* Yes, to yourself. You look surprised; but I mean what I say. All my money, amounting to more than £20,000, shall be yours, upon one condition; and that is, if you will *marry my grand-daughter.*"

"Marry your grand-daughter? why, she is a mere child, if you mean the one I have seen here with you."

"Annie is just fourteen. See that she is educated; get Lady De Marbury to act as her guardian;

and, in three or four years' time, she will be fit to be the wife even of a De Marbury."

Sir John was too much astounded at the proposition to be able to say more than—

"I must think this well over, and you shall have my answer as soon as possible. My mother is now on a visit with me, and I shall lose no time in consulting her about your offer."

"And, Sir John," went on the old man, detaining him as he was rising to take his leave, "remember that my days are counted—nay, that it may be a question of hours with me. Tarry not, then, and let me have your answer before twelve o'clock to-morrow."

"Depend on me. Does your grand-daughter know anything of this?"

"Not a syllable."

Sir John encountered the unconscious subject of this conversation as he went down-stairs and passed through the hall, or passage, leading to the front door. She was looking smiling and pleasant as usual, and courtesied, as was her wont, as the young baronet prepared to pass through the door which she held open for him. Not a trace of consciousness appeared on her features—not the faintest surmise that she was looking, it might be, upon her future husband. She had never spoken to her grandfather's titled visitor in her life, but had only smiled and courtesied as she had answered the door once or twice, and let him in or out. So it was a surprise to her that Sir John should, upon this occasion, and contrary to what had ever happened before, stop for a few moments to express his concern at her grandfather's illness. He was curious to hear the sound of her voice, to observe her manner. "If she *is* to be my wife, it is time that I should know something about her," he said to himself. But there was not much to be got out of Annie. Ideas do not flow very fast, or words come readily, to a little maiden of fourteen, addressed for the first time in her life by a handsome young man of two or three and twenty—vastly her superior in station, the owner of Donnington Hall, the place her grandfather was so fond of talking about. Sir John, too, spoke to her with more of feeling and personal interest than was usually

addressed to her by those in his station. This, however, she put down in her own mind to his being
such a "nice gentleman; so free, too." She said,
however, but little—only looked her thanks; and Sir
John took his departure, almost knocking against
Tom Swigmore, who, since the old man's attack,
had kept hovering about the house in case he
should be wanted. He considered that Sir John's
unusually late visit must have reference to himself—perhaps he was to be his guardian. And
so he was not a little disappointed as the baronet
passed him without saying a word, but only
returned Tom's salute.

The nature of the decision come to by Sir John
De Marbury and his mother on the subject which
occupied, as may be supposed, their entire thoughts,
and formed the chief subject of their conversation
that evening and the following morning, might
have been surmised by the appearance of the Donnington carriage in the streets of Newchurch early
on the day succeeding the conversation with the
old man. In this carriage were seated Lady De
Marbury and Sir John. The carriage drove at

once through one or two back streets and then was drawn up at Jacob Delves's door. A hurried glance up at the windows, as they got out, assured the visitors that the old man was still in the land of the living. Sir John at once went up-stairs, and was soon closeted with him, while Lady De Marbury, asking to be shown into the sitting-room, sent a message by the female who opened the door —a neighbour's wife, come in to help—with a request that she might speak with the grand-daughter. And Annie, accordingly, soon made her appearance at the summons. It was evident from her demeanour that she had not the slightest conception of the real object Lady De Marbury had in view in wishing to see her. She first thought that it must be about a " place " for her when her grand-father was dead ; perhaps Lady De Marbury was going to have her about her own person, to train her to be her maid after a while. And this, she thought, would be so pleasant—far preferable to having to live with one of her aunts, and to have to work hard for a living. Then, she thought, when she observed Lady De Marbury's grave, quiet manner, as, after looking at her attentively, she said to her, on entering the room, " Come here, my dear, and sit beside me. I want you to like me ; and I am sure, from your face, that I shall be very fond of you after a time." She thought that this great lady must have heard something about her, and was going to give her some good advice ; perhaps it was to caution her against Tom Swigmore. This was the only thing she could think of. What was, then, her overwhelming astonishment when Lady De Marbury said to her, in the kindest and gentlest of tones—

" Annie, love, your grandfather made a proposal to my son yesterday, which greatly concerns yourself, and it is about that proposal I am come to speak to you. You must be very calm, my dear, while I am telling you what that proposal is, and you must try and consider me as if I was your mother, and not be at all afraid to open your mind to me. Your grandfather, then, wishes that you should become my son's wife—that you should be Lady De Marbury—and offers to endow you with almost all his fortune if his wishes are gratified.

Of course, Annie, though the marriage ceremony would be performed without delay, for your poor grandfather's satisfaction before he died, yet you would not go and live at the Hall, or with Sir John as his wife, until three or four years had elapsed. You would be sent to school, in the first instance, to be educated. And then you would come and live with me until you were properly trained and qualified to take your place in the world as Lady De Marbury, and to be the mistress of Donnington Hall. Now tell me, my love, what you think of such a change in your prospects."

Annie had a tender, sensitive disposition; and so, after making several attempts to answer Lady De Marbury, she at length fairly broke down and burst into tears. She sobbed hysterically for a considerable time, and allowed Lady De Marbury to soothe and quiet her as if she was her own mother. At length, after a considerable interval, she was just able to articulate, " Oh, what happiness may be in store for me !" and then had to beg that she might be allowed to retire to her room and lie down a little. And so, with a parting kiss from Lady De Marbury, little Annie retired, just too as Sir John's steps were heard upon the stairs. Mother and son shortly afterwards quitted the house, and, entering into the carriage, which they found waiting at the door, drove out to Donnington. When in the carriage, Sir John recounted what had passed between himself and the old man. He had found Jacob much the same; and, upon communicating to him the acceptance of the offer, the old man's countenance had quite brightened up. He said, " I shall live, then, to see a grandchild of mine after all mistress of Donnington ! who could ever have thought of such a thing! when I have once seen *that* secured, I care not how soon I go." Most of their conversation then turned, Sir John said, upon the arrangements that would be necessary in order to carry out the plan. Amongst other things, it was settled that Sir John should proceed at once to London on that very afternoon, procure a special license from the Archbishop of Canterbury, granting a dispensation as to hours and places, and that the ceremony should be performed on the following evening, by the sick man's bedside. Detaining the carriage, then, at the door, when they reached the Hall, Sir John just went in to get the few things necessary for his journey, and drove off to the nearest station, which he reached in time for the up express train.

## CHAPTER XIV.

IT was evening. Jacob Delves lay dying. A mournful group were gathered about his bedside. The doctor, Mr. Wright, was in and out of the room occasionally. His patient, he said, could not last through the night. But for stimulants, he would probably have passed away ere this. The old man lay perfectly composed; his breathing was easier. Nought was heard but an occasional whisper from one of the attendant group to the other. That group consisted of little Annie, who, with head buried in her hands, was kneeling by the bedside, one of her aged grandfather's cold hands clasped in hers and moistened with her tears.

Lady De Marbury sat by the dying man's

pillow, and read to him, every now and then,
a verse out of the Book of Comfort. The curate
of the parish, Mr. Jackson, had but an hour
or two previously administered to him the most
solemn of all religious rites, the Holy Communion,
and he was now in an adjoining room, conversing
in an under-tone with the doctor; he had been
requested to wait, as his services might be required
again very shortly. A hired nurse, and a neighbour, moved about the sick room with noiseless
feet to get anything that was required. Old
Jacob's wants were now few enough, it was plain.
He occasionally opened his eyes, however, and
seemed to fix them upon the kneeling figure by
his bedside, from whom a sob of anguish would
escape at intervals. Lady De Marbury was composed and tranquil, as usual, though her face wore
traces of recent weeping. She looked at her
watch occasionally, and seemed to be expecting
somebody.

As the evening wore on and turned into night
some anxiety began to betray itself in her usually
placid features. She spoke in a whisper to the

doctor each time he approached the bedside, which he began to do at more frequent intervals than before, and appeared uneasy at the dubious expression of his countenance. "He is sinking fast," at length he said, almost out loud. Jacob did not, as heretofore, open his eyes or take the least notice of the interruption to the prevailing silence; but, just at that moment, and as Lady De Marbury was smoothing the pillow of death, the sound of wheels was heard under the window, and of a horse being pulled up suddenly with a jerk. The nurse's assistant quietly left the room. There was a sound as of an arrival down-stairs, and presently the female returned, and, whispering a few words to the clergyman, who was standing by the bedside, having just finished the commendatory prayer for one about to depart, withdrew him from the room.

The slight noise below seemed to have had the effect of arousing Jacob; he opened his eyes again, and they seemed to follow the retreating figure of the clergyman. He murmured something which Lady De Marbury in vain

endeavoured to catch.    Presently the same female
attendant touched Annie on the shoulder, who
arose and followed her out of the room.    A small
table with a white cloth on it, which had been
used at the administration of the Holy Communion,
and which stood in a corner of the room, was now
brought forward by the nurse and placed at the
foot of the bed, and a few simple arrangements
made for the performance of some ceremony.    The
effect produced upon Jacob had been quite mar-
vellous.    He watched the arrangements with
something of his former intelligence.    "It has
recalled him to life for the time," said the surgeon,
turning to Lady De Marbury; "but, when the
little excitement is over, he will pass away."    The
small table arranged, there was a slight sound
outside the door, as of two or three assembling in
the passage, and immediately afterwards the clergyman entered, wearing his surplice, and took his
place at one end of the little table, and so as to
stand sideways towards the dying man.

Sir John De Marbury next came in, accompanied by his solicitor, Mr. Ardern, and at once

handed to the officiating minister what looked like a slip of parchment with a large seal dangling to it, and which proved to be a special license from the most Reverend Father in God, William, by Divine Providence, Lord Archbishop of Canterbury, authorizing his beloved in Christ, Henry William Jackson, Clerk, Master of Arts, Curate of Newchurch, or any other lawful minister, to celebrate a marriage between one John De Marbury, of the parish of Donnington, in the county of Chester, Baronet, a bachelor, and of full age (as asserted), and one Ann Eckersley (otherwise Delves), of the parish of Newchurch, in the same county, spinster, and dispensing, by virtue of the prerogative now and from ancient times attached to the see of Canterbury, and for due and sufficient reasons set forth in the affidavit of the above-named John De Marbury, Baronet, with the observance of canonical hours, and permitting the marriage to be performed in any fit place other than a duly licensed church or chapel.

The clergyman just glanced at this document, and then, laying it down, and opening his book, prepared to read the service. Lady De Marbury had gone out of the room, but returned in two or three minutes leading Annie Delves by the hand. The attendant had thrown over Annie a white muslin scarf or mantle, but, with this exception, she wore the same simple cotton dress that she usually did.

Sir John had not seen her since he spoke those few words to her at the door on the night of his visit to Jacob, and partly turned towards her, as if to greet her, when his mother conducted her in and placed her on the left hand of her son. The medical man remained standing by Jacob, occasionally turning aside to observe the group at that little table. The nurse was entirely occupied in watching Jacob, moistening his lips from time to time, and administering a teaspoonful of weak brandy-and-water occasionally.

There was a perfect silence in the room for a minute or two, and then fell upon the ears of all present those solemn, affecting words which are rehearsed to us at the most momentous period of our lives—"Dearly beloved, we are gathered together here in the sight of God, and in the face of this congregation, to join together this man and this woman in holy matrimony;" and so on with the remainder of the address. When the question was put, "Who giveth this woman to be married to this man?" there was a hesitation for a moment, when Mr. Ardern stepped forward, and, taking Annie's hand, placed it in that of her future husband. Sir John went calmly through his part, and repeated the necessary words after the minister in a low but distinct voice, adapted to the place where they were assembled. As for Annie, it was in tones faltering with emotion, though heard in the stillness of that chamber of death, that she repeated after the clergyman, "I, Annie, take thee, John, to my wedded husband," &c. "The ring?" whispered the clergyman to Sir John; but this was the first time he remembered such a thing would be wanted. His mother, however, quietly slipping off her own wedding ring, supplied the deficiency. The remaining part of the service (with abridgments)

N

was then proceeded with. At its conclusion, first Sir John, and next Lady De Marbury, imprinted a kiss on the bride's forehead; and then they all approached the bedside of the dying man.

"Do you know what has been passing?" the clergyman asked of Jacob.

"Yes," he whispered; "God bless you all. I am going." He then stretched out his withered arms, and, taking Sir John's hand and Annie's in his, and clasping them together, said, "I now die happy: Lord receive my spirit!" And with these words old Jacob Delves fell back into the arms of Lady De Marbury, and passed out of life without a groan or struggle. The little family party—that is, mother, son, and daughter-in-law —assembled in the sitting-room, leaving the attendants to perform the customary sad offices for the dead.

"My dear, dear daughter," exclaimed Lady De Marbury, with considerable emotion, as she embraced the weeping Annie, and sought to comfort her, "you have lost one parent, but you have gained another; and especially you will be the object of my son's tenderest love and affection when the time comes for surrendering up my charge." With these and such like fond maternal expressions did Lady De Marbury soothe the troubled mind of her youthful daughter-in-law. When Annie grew more composed, plans began to be discussed, Sir John striking in occasionally, and adopting a cheerful and encouraging, rather than tender or sentimental, manner towards his child-wife. By degrees little Annie's smiles came again, and she was able to take some part, and show an interest, in the conversation that followed.

"You will return with me, my love, to the Hall to-night. I have ordered the carriage to be here in half-an-hour's time, and you can put up the few things you will want. We shall stay at the Hall until after the funeral, which will take place at Donnington, and which we shall all attend. You will have time against then to have your mourning made up, and to be provided with such things as you require. For, immediately after the funeral, we leave for Bath;

and there, my love, I hope to make arrangements
for putting you to some first-rate school.   But all
these after-arrangements we shall have plenty of
time to discuss at Donnington.   Now wish your
husband good-bye for the present : he will stop at
Mr. Ardern's for a day or two, and then goes to
Ashton Hall until after the funeral.   But here
comes the carriage."

Annie's simple preparations did not occupy
much time, and, handed into the carriage by Sir
John, both mother and daughter-in-law were soon
on the road to Donnington Hall.   As Sir John
was leaving the house, having given what directions he deemed necessary, he was accosted, in a
somewhat familiar tone, by Tom Swigmore, who
had, apparently, been drinking.

" So the poor old man is gone at last—thought
he'd have sent for me.   'Pon honour, a shame for
a man to neglect his nephew at such a time!
Hope, however, he has made up for it in his will.
Perhaps you can tell me, Sir John, as you have
been so *uncommonly* attentive to the old man, how
my uncle has left his money ?"

" I believe," said Sir John, speaking with forced civility, "that the will is in Mr. Ardern's hands, and that it will not be read until after the funeral. I am not able, therefore, to tell you anything about it."

" Oh, that's it," said the young man, with an impertinent sneer. " I suppose I musn't ask you, then, if you know its contents ?"

" You may ask, certainly," was Sir John's reply, as he lighted a cigar, " but I shall take the liberty of refusing to give you any answer."

" Oh, indeed ! and I suppose I am not to know where Annie is gone to either ?"

" She is gone home with Lady De Marbury —I have no objection to tell you *that*—and will be well cared for in future."

" I never heard of such a thing ! *My* mother and aunt are her nearest relations, and ought to have the charge of her, I know that."

" It is at her grandfather's special request, and by his directions, that your cousin has been placed under my mother's charge."

Muttering to himself that he wasn't going to be

" done out of his rights in that way by all the De
Marburys in England," this hopeful young man
took his departure, while Sir John pursued his
way to Mr. Ardern's.

At Jacob's express request, his funeral was conducted in the most unostentatious manner. He
was buried in the place indicated by himself, Mr.
Hulton reading the burial service. No invitations
to the funeral were issued; but it was thought
right to intimate the hour that had been fixed on
to the near relations of Jacob, who resided in and
about Newchurch. Accordingly, most of them
attended. It was made known, also, that, after
the service, and at the school-house, the will would
be read by Mr. Ardern.

The hour fixed for the funeral was twelve
o'clock; and shortly before that time Lady
De Marbury, accompanied by Annie, arrived
from the Hall, and fell in with the line of
mourners as they entered the churchyard, Sir
John taking his place as chief mourner. After
the service, the whole party adjourned to the
school-room to hear the will read. It was very

short. £100 was bequeathed to each of the sisters, and £50 apiece to the children; £200 was left to the vicar and churchwardens of Donnington for ever, the interest of which was to be distributed every Christmas in coals and warm clothing amongst the poor. All the residue of his property he bequeathed to his grand-daughter, Annie Eckersley, otherwise Delves, appointing Sir John De Marbury as her sole guardian, and directing that she should live with Lady De Marbury until she attained the age of seventeen years. He also appointed Sir John as his sole executor and trustee. This was the will. A dead silence succeeded the reading of it; until, at length, one of the sisters, pushing back her chair, and exclaiming that " she didn't see what was to be got by remaining there," prepared the way for a general move on the part of the re- lations. Tom, judging from his countenance, was boiling over with indignation, but deeming it safest, apparently, to refrain from giving expression to it until he had got outside the door, and out of the presence of those " nobs " (so he designated Sir John, the rector, and Mr. Ardern), he said nothing

until he joined the group of aunts and cousins,
but was then heard, with a loud voice, to intimate
his opinion that " he knew who had got round the
old man," and that "anything more iniquitous "
he (Tom) had " never heard of."

Of course the fact of Sir John's marriage
very soon oozed out; and so he was not surprised, upon entering the Rectory, to receive
at once Mr. Hulton's friendly, good-humoured
congratulations, delivered in an under‑tone.
There was luncheon prepared; and Annie had
turned to such good account the few days that
she had already spent at the Hall, and her
mourning became her so well, that Sir John had
no reason to be ashamed of the appearance or
manners of his child-wife, even sitting, as she was,
beside Mrs. Hulton herself. After all the occurrences of the last ten days, and the consequent
excitement, the rest of the Rectory was pronounced
a real enjoyment; and, as Sir John strolled with
Annie about the beautifully laid out grounds, and
as he talked to her of their future plans, when she
would come to reside at the Hall, an increased

feeling of satisfaction stole over him, and he felt
how tenderly he could love the simple, artless child
of nature walking beside him, and resolved that
her future happiness should be his study. Sir
John then bade adieu to her, and they did not
meet again for three years.

## CHAPTER XV.

WITHIN a few hours' sail of the English shores are a group of islands which are scarcely as much visited as might have been expected. For, whereas tourists on the Continent and up the Rhine may be reckoned by the hundred, visitors to the Channel Islands are to be told off by dozens. The mixture of races, and the blending of home with Continental customs, give a charm to Jersey and Guernsey in particular, which is not to be found elsewhere. The natives are singularly tenacious of their rights and peculiar customs; and, though largely indebted to the strangers who visit, or have taken up their abode on, these islands, yet little intercourse prevails between the two. These islanders are indeed unparalleled in their own conceit. They consider that England belongs to them, not they to England; and, in the case even of outrages on the person or property (so as the person aggrieved be not a native of the island—which makes all the difference, as you will find out if you try), the ends of justice are considered to be sufficiently answered by the "transportation" of the criminal "*to England,*" to Ireland—wherever he likes to go. Banishment from one of these sweet islands is punishment enough, in the Jerseyman's opinion, for all but the worst class of offences; and, even in the case of these, where the prosecutor, suppose, is an Englishman, and the defendant is a Jerseyman, it is useless to go into their courts of law, where all the proceedings are carried on in Norman-French —where the judges, the advocates, the jurats, all the officials, are natives. You may possibly procure a conviction where the evidence is overwhelming (such a thing has been known); but as for seeing the sentence carried out, as for seeing a Jerseyman sent to prison on your account—an Englishman, as you are—you must put that out

of your head. It is not to be thought of for
a single moment. Be content if your enemy
is willing to let you have your property back
again, or if he promises to assault you no more,
and go your way. Let it be a lesson to you not
to go to law with a Jerseyman again. It must be
admitted, however, in fairness, that no complaint
on the score of tardiness of justice can be made in
cases the reverse of this, where the Jerseyman is
the plaintiff and you are the defendant. For so
swiftly does the arm of the law reach you, that an
affidavit on the part of the plaintiff that *he thinks*
you are likely to leave the island is quite enough
to insure your incarceration *sine die*. You are
arrested with very little ceremony and thrown
into prison, and what becomes of you afterwards it
matters not now to speculate about. Even the
Queen's writ is hardly obeyed in these very inde-
pendent islands; and we know that a few years
ago there was a regular trial of strength between
the Court of Queen's Bench and the Supreme
Court of Jersey, which ended in a kind of drawn
battle.

Despite these drawbacks, however, Jersey and Guernsey are pleasant places enough to visit, if not to reside in. Few of us have any occasion to go into their courts of law. As we know what awaits us there, we had better keep out of them, and settle that little matter of ours with Le Breton or De Journeaux out of doors. But we all appreciate pure air and charming scenery. And these you have to perfection in the two islands I am principally referring to. Grapes ripen in the open air; and in no part of Devon or Cornwall do the myrtles, fuchsias, and geraniums flourish more, or attain a greater height. Jersey pears have a world-wide reputation; and equally plentiful and fine are most of the other fruits, such as peaches and nectarines, which find their way over in such abundance from the sunny slopes of Brittany and Normandy, which lie before you dazzling in the sun. Walk into the market of St. Hélier on a Saturday; listen to the jabbering of French (or what passes for such) going on; see those Norman peasants with their snowy white caps, some of them towering in the

air like helmets,—and you might well fancy yourself in some foreign market-place. And as for
the Jersey and Guernsey lanes, what visitor can
have forgotten their peculiar charm?—narrow,
with steep banks covered with flowers, and the
trees arched overhead, with glimpses of the sea
occasionally; and then those exquisitely cultivated little fields and well-kept orchards, and the
graceful little Jersey cow tethered amidst rich
pastures. Altogether, the interior of these islands
presents a scene of rural beauty and rich cultivation seldom to be met with anywhere else. The
same subdivision of land which exists now in
France prevails also in Jersey and Guernsey;
and, whatever may be thought of its effects on a
larger scale, yet, in a little island, and amongst a
primitive people whose wants are few and who
live sparingly, such a system seems to work well,
as it certainly conduces to the rich, highly
cultivated appearance of the two islands. Every
peasant almost has his plot of ground—frequently
his cow—and what between supplying the markets
of St. Hélier and St. Peter's Port, in both which

towns there is a large English population, and
selling his milk and butter, he seems to thrive
well enough. Except on government works, and
in the nursery-gardens, there is but little constant
employment to be had in these two islands.
There are, indeed, several dreary manor-houses,
surrounded with a few trees, to be found scattered
up and down ; but they seem to be generally shut
up or unoccupied. The contrast between these
dark gloomy demesnes, with their dilapidated
gates—off their hinges probably—and the window-
shut house, with those smiling green pastures,
and rich orchards, and extensive fields of parsnips
and carrots (on which the cattle are fed), is
striking indeed. And as for the lord, the
" Seigneur," as he is called, he is nobody, never
seen or heard of, and possessed of no influence in
the island. The subdivision of land has worked
ill for *him*, it must be admitted, as it has for the
descendants of the old *noblesse* in France. For
what is a " Seigneur" without tenants and de-
pendants ?—what but a vain and empty name ?

In the chief town of Jersey, St. Hélier, and in

its immediate neighbourhood, there are a great
many English and Irish families of respectability
resident.   The society to be had there, and the
supposed cheapness of the living, together with
educational advantages, constitute the chief attraction.   Climate and scenery allure more ephe-
meral visitors.   At any rate, what between
visitors and residents, the English and Irish in
St. Hélier far outnumber the natives; and, as
they bring with them their own habits and
customs, and see much to object to in the
laws and government of the little island, and
make frequent efforts to correct what they deem
amiss, it may be supposed that the regard entertained towards them by the natives, high and low,
is the very reverse of enthusiastic or demon-
strative.

However, the Jerseyman likes the Englishman's
gold, if he does not like himself; and the Englishman likes the island, though he can make nothing
of the natives; and so they get on together some-
how.   There are crescents and terraces without
end in the immediate vicinity of the town, and,

a little farther out in the country, though still quite within a walk, old-fashioned châteaus and farm-houses.

In one of these châteaus, about a mile from the town, two ladies had been resident for some months in the summer of 184—. They might be mother and daughter, to judge from their probable ages. They walked and drove about the island like other people, but kept no society. As there was an extensive flower-garden in front of the house, the younger of the two ladies seemed to fill up her time with her flowers and plants; and occasionally she, as well as her companion, would sit and read under one of the many wide-spreading chestnut-trees which were in the neighbourhood of the house. The house itself had, in its time, been probably the residence of some family of note. The floors were all of dark polished oak, or more probably walnut, with a wide staircase to correspond; and in more than one of the principal rooms the oak panelling had been preserved. Vines, and jessamine, and other creeping plants covered the sides of the house in rich profusion.  Altogether, a pleasanter or more picturesque temporary abode Lady De Marbury —or rather Annie, for she it was who at once set her heart upon securing the place—could not well have pitched upon.  They had had plenty of knocking about, had these two ladies, and were glad enough now of a little repose during the short time longer they were to remain together.

Three years and upwards had elapsed since those two ladies had looked upon Sir John's face, and since they bade him farewell in the hall of Donnington Rectory.  Two of those years had been spent in Bath and London, where Sir John's wife had every advantage in the shape of instruction and masters that money could procure ; and the last year had been spent entirely on the Continent, first at Paris, and subsequently at Rome and Florence.

They had not very long returned from their travels, and here in Jersey it was fixed that the meeting so long planned, and so often and so anxiously thought about, should take place.

Sir John had been a still greater traveller than themselves. Where had he not been? He had been to Constantinople, Greece, Egypt, the Holy Land, all over the East almost. Returning occasionally to Donnington, yet he had never remained at home long together since the departure of his mother and her charge. His position when at home was not exactly an agreeable one—married, and yet a single man, as it were. By those of his own age and condition he would be bantered not a little about his child-wife. Young ladies would amuse themselves at his expense, and could not always refrain from a sly question or innuendo bearing upon his matrimonial circumstances; while grave old country squires and plotting mammas would, by their studied silence, and avoidance of anything bearing upon the subject, seem to intimate their opinion that Sir John had made a *mésalliance*, in some degree compromising, not only himself, but his "order"—necessary, it might be, but still to be regretted.

There was not much temptation then for

Sir John to remain at home.  He found that
both Sessions and agricultural meetings could
go on very well without him, that his law
began to be sneered at, his knowledge of agri-
culture to be altogether disbelieved in.   Even
Mrs. Hulton slightly " patronized" him, and had
the pleasure of announcing to him (which we may
be sure she did with no sort of reluctance) Lotty's
engagement to young Lord Harecastle, and of
dwelling upon the many admirable qualities of
which the youthful peer was supposed to be the
possessor.

Altogether, Sir John was glad enough to start
off on another continental ramble, this time fully
intending to make the ascent of Mont Blanc (not
such a common feat then as it has become since) and
to take up his residence at Geneva.   He had been
absent on this last occasion upwards of a twelve-
month, and was now daily expected.   It was
agreed that he was to join his mother and wife in
Jersey, and, after staying some time in that island,
that he should return to Donnington with his
bride and introduce her to the county.   The time

was over-due when they might expect Sir John, and each morning, when the ladies awoke, they anticipated the probability of seeing him before night.

It was an anxious time for the younger of the two. During those three years that had gone over her head since her grandfather's death she had passed from almost childhood to woman-hood—from the condition of a peasant-girl, it might be said, to a rank and station that would place her on terms of equality with the proudest in the land.

"Will he be pleased with me? Will he be satisfied with my looks? Is there anything about my manners he would wish different?" These were the questions the young girl would put to herself as she stood before the glass arranging her golden tresses as they fell in rich profusion over her shoulders.

Annie had shot up now into a tall, graceful woman: she had just enough colour to denote perfect health; and her large, liquid, dark eyes would be lighted up with animation when talking upon any subject that interested her. She was very lively and unaffected, and recurred to her early days, when there was any occasion for it, in a simple, modest manner. From the very first she had looked up to Lady De Marbury, and quite treated her as if she had been her own mother; and, now that the time was approaching when they must be separated, each thought of the inevitable event with a pang, and almost regretted that another year of preparation could not be added to its predecessors.

In a delightful climate like that of Jersey, and during the summer months, a drive to the sea-side is always a pleasant mode of passing the day; and you have your choice of a number of delightful places — Mt. Orgueil, St. Catherine's, Roselle, Goree, and many other equally charming spots.

Of these places, Roselle was, perhaps, the favourite with Annie and her mother, as she now always called Lady De Marbury; and they would delight to start early from Rougemont Farm (for so was the place called where they resided), and, taking refreshments with them, to bring their books and work, and to spend the day at Roselle, choosing some pleasant spot commanding a good view of the sea and of the opposite coast of France; or sometimes Annie would bring her drawing materials and make a sketch of any picturesque object— a sail-boat, a Jersey peasant in her red petticoat and *sabots*.

They had driven out one day, as usual, and were partly working, partly talking. The opposite coast would seem to have suggested the same line of thought to both.

"I wonder when we shall see John," Lady De Marbury said, "and where he is now."

"I was just thinking about it. He must, one would think, have crossed over to England, or he would have been here before this : he was to have left Geneva, you know, several days ago."

"Why, he knows that there are steamers direct to Jersey from St. Malo and Granville, and it is more likely he will come by one of them. There may have been some delay."

"Well, we shall know all about it soon ;" and

Annie proceeded to arrange some flowers they had been given from a neighbouring garden.

"You shall know all about it now, if you like," said a voice close to them, and Sir John De Marbury, with delight written on his face, stood before them.

"Well, John, we were just talking about you, and wondering what had become of you. Where have you dropped from?"

Lady De Marbury spoke in her usual conversational tone, as if she had only parted from her son the day before. She thus gave Annie time to get over any feeling of nervousness or emotion which the sudden appearance of her husband might have occasioned.

"Why," said Sir John, "I have been most vexatiously detained at Granville these couple of days, owing to some accident to the steamer. Its engines were out of order; and there I have been kept waiting on, in that dullest of all towns, where there is nothing but the church to look at. I should think you might almost see it from here, for it stands conspicuously on a hill. What a charming look-out you have from here! Well, Annie, would you have known me again? I should have passed you, I declare: you have grown a great deal."

It was in this easy chatty way the first meeting was got over, so anxiously looked forward to by all parties. Actually, Annie had not to make a single one of the many pretty speeches she had prepared in her own mind for the first occasion on which she should meet her husband after such a long separation! Nor had he looked at her in the least as she expected, or made any remark or put any such questions as she thought. He hardly looked at her at first, as he sat down on the grass beside them; and it was not until they had been chatting and laughing together for some time that she became aware she was the object of his quiet but earnest scrutiny.

"Well, you want to know how I found you out here," he went on gaily, replying to a question of Annie's. "Why, we got into the harbour very early this morning, and, as I couldn't think of knocking you up at such an unconscionable hour, I made for the hotel, turned in, and had a good sleep, and then, after a cup of coffee and a biscuit, I set off to find you. It was some time before I could make out whereabouts Rouge-mont Farm lay; and then I took two or three wrong turns; so that it was after eleven when I got to the house, fully expecting to see you both. Just fancy my disappointment when your servant told me that you had both gone out for the day, and were not expected back until evening! Luckily, she was able to tell me where you had gone, or I should have been distracted: I posi-tively should, Mrs. Annie, though you laugh so. Well, then, I posted back to the hotel, got a horse, and here I am, as hungry as possible. However, I have brought some sandwiches in my pocket, not wishing to take you at an unfair advantage."

"It is well you have, John; for I don't suppose Capel (she is my new maid) has put up much more in the basket than is sufficient for Annie and myself."

Sitting down on the grass, then, and enjoying

the pure air and stretch of blue sea before them, they partook of such provisions as were to be had.

Sir John was in raptures with the scenery. "I saw 'Lodgings' stuck up in one of the windows of that house with the pretty garden before it as I came along. What do you say, both of you, to our coming out here for two or three weeks?"

"Well, Annie and I have been talking about it more than once; we are both so fond of this spot; and I think you two young people can't do better than come out and stay here for two or three weeks. It is just the place to spend one's honeymoon."

"What do you say, Annie?" asked her husband.

Annie blushed considerably, but she thought "it would be a very nice place to stay at," only Lady De Marbury must come too. "It would be pleasant," she added, "for us all to be together."

However, her ladyship was not to be persuaded. "She would drive out and see them frequently," she said, "but she would be *de trop* staying with them at present. No; she would stop at home

and take care of Rougemont; and when they were
tired of each other's company they were to come
to her."

And thus it was settled. The "lodgings" were
taken, and were to be ready against next day; and
so the party drove home, Sir John sending the
horse back by one of the helpers from a neighbouring inn.

## CHAPTER XVI.

THERE was this peculiarity in the relationship between Sir John De Marbury and Annie, that though in one sense an "old" married couple, yet that in reality they were all but strangers to each other. He had never been half an hour alone in her company in his life. They had corresponded, indeed; but Sir John was not much of a letter-writer, so his effusions were principally protestations of undying love whenever they should come to live together; while *hers* savoured too much of the boarding-school young lady. She did not, in fact, well know what to put in them. It hardly seemed maidenly to dwell too much upon her love for him, a stranger to her almost; and anything short of that—regard, esteem, affection,

what not—seemed tame and unsatisfactory.   Lady
De Marbury, to whom she once casually mentioned
her difficulty, could give her but little assistance.
She thought all love-letters a pack of nonsense—
by long-established prescription—and that it did
not much matter how many terms of endearment
you crammed into them.   They were all words, of
course ; a few, more or less, what did it signify ?
Still this did not relieve Annie's perplexity : she
could never write a letter to her husband to her
satisfaction.

"Give him an account, my dear, as minute as
you like," said Lady De Marbury to her, one day,
seeing the half-filled sheet of paper before her, and
the writer apparently at a complete stand-still, "of
the places you have visited, of the people you have
met, of the books you are reading : this will always
fill up your letters, and the time will, after all, be
better employed than in dwelling on all your little
hopes and fears and phantasies."

The advice was taken ; and, accordingly, much
to Sir John's amusement, who partly guessed the
cause, his wife's letters were in future almost

entirely taken up with lively sketches of where
they had been, whom they had met, and, when
very hard driven indeed for a subject (for her
husband seldom looked at anything but a newspaper), what books she had been reading; and
the change was altogether to be commended, for
Annie wrote freely and naturally upon subjects
she was at home in.

Again, though both so young, yet there was a
difference of nearly ten years between them, which
told for something in their intercourse. Sir John,
too, had been always, in Annie's eyes, the Squire
of Donnington, the most influential man about
Newchurch, and she had never known him in any
other light. How was she, then, to look upon him
as her husband, how to pet and caress him, how
to tease and tantalize him—all of which have been
the privileges of a wife from time immemorial, as
Annie knew very well, by a kind of instinct, I believe? She felt as if she could hardly ever be quite
at her ease with him. Even his frank, careless,
joyous manner, when he came upon them so unexpectedly at Roselle, did not quite remove all her

tremors at once, though his manner was certainly reassuring.

But now the time had come for her to assume her position as the wife of Sir John De Marbury; and wisely did the old lady pack them both off to Roselle, to get acquainted with each other, and to shake off that feeling of strangeness which must necessarily cling to them both for a while.

They were left to their own resources for a good week, notwithstanding the motherly promise of frequent visits; and that week had wrought wonders. When Lady De Marbury paid them a visit her daughter-in-law could order her husband about, could rally him about his old loves (she had already possessed herself of the particulars respecting Miss Lotty, and took a dislike at once to that young lady, to which she gave free expression occasionally), and altogether had her husband in as good training as if she had known him for years, and to an extent that rather astonished her mother-in-law.

"No occasion," was her mental reflection, "to make myself uneasy about their not getting on."

"I have just been telling John," said the lively young lady, as she presided at the head of her own table, "that he smokes a great deal too much, and that I mean to limit him to two or three cigars in the course of the day. Don't you think I am quite right, mamma? See how his hand shakes; and that is all from smoking so much, I know it is."

"I suppose I picked up the habit in the East. They do nothing else there, scarcely, but smoke."

"Your poor father was very seldom without a cigar in his mouth, and I am afraid he injured his health by that means. So I think you are quite right, Annie, to try and induce John to leave off smoking."

"Oh, I won't be so hard upon him as all that, poor fellow! but I'll keep his cigars for him, and only give him one now and then when he deserves it—when he behaves properly;" and here the young lady gave a would-be saucy look at her husband, who paid her off presently after a fashion that is common enough amongst newly-married

P

couples, and which occasionally causes a slight degree of embarrassment on the part of the lookers-on. However, the mother was most obligingly blind; and were they not both her children? "Only," she thought to herself, "in *my* time young people were much more on their guard." It was with difficulty the young couple could tear themselves away from so sweet and pleasant a retreat.

The frequent visits of strangers, too, who are sure to pay Roselle a visit during their stay in Jersey, prevented the place from appearing dull. The infinite variety of costumes adopted by English tourists—the caps and wide-awakes, of all shapes and colours—is amusing enough, and afforded frequent employment for Annie's pencil, when inclined to sketch.

She was amusing herself one day transferring to paper a more than ordinary John-Bullish-looking person, very stout and red-faced, with white hat and in a suit of nankeen, and was touching off his great clumsy feet, so as to give her husband a good laugh when he joined her. He was coming up to where she was sitting, a little apart, upon a camp-stool, and the group of which the subject of her sketch formed one were at a little distance off dispersed about, and waiting apparently until divers imposing-looking hampers were unpacked.

"Why, that is old Legh, as I am alive! Where were your eyes? You must have seen him often in Newchurch. Ah, Legh, what brings you here?"

"Bless my soul, De Marbury, is that you?" and the two shook hands cordially.

Annie's sketch, we may be sure, disappeared rapidly enough within the recesses of her portfolio, and she had hardly accomplished this manœuvre when her husband brought up his friend to introduce him.

The old gentleman, at first, could hardly credit that the tall and elegant-looking young lady whom he had observed sketching—little suspecting, however, the subject of her drawing—was none other than old Jacob Delves's grand-daughter, and the wife of his friend and

neighbour Sir John De Marbury.   He was a
courteous and polite old man, grotesque as he
looked in the dress in which he had thought fit to
array himself, and which was as different as possible
from anything he ever thought of wearing when
at home.   So, approaching Annie, and taking her
hand after quite a paternal fashion, he said, " I
am proud indeed to make the acquaintance of my
friend's wife.   I knew your grandfather very well
indeed, and we have often had a chat together.
How long have you been in Jersey?" &c., &c.;
and so the ice was broken, and Annie and the old
gentleman talked away as if they had been old
friends.   And it was only when the calls and
summonses to the old gentleman from his party
became too urgent to be any longer disregarded
with safety, that he and the De Marburys bade
adieu to each other.

"We shall hope to be amongst the very
first to pay our respects at Donnington Hall
when we all find our way back into Cheshire;"
these were the kind old man's parting words.

Another week was to be spent by them in

Jersey, not at Roselle any longer, but at Rouge-
mont Farm with the elder Lady De Marbury, and
then the young couple thought of turning their
faces homewards.

St. Hélier is a great *rendezvous* of retired military
and naval men. Generals, and colonels, and admirals
are to be met with there as thick as blackberries.
You are perpetually, when walking in the streets,
knocking against ex-governors, and former commanding officers of regiments. The little comforts
and luxuries of life which such extinguished
potentates and deposed rulers especially affect,
such as French wines, and brandies, and grapes,
and pine-apples, are to be had in great plenty and
abundance, and cheap, upon the island. No one
ever dreams of setting up an equipage in Jersey.
So that, though in England it might excite remark to see the ex-Governor of Timbuctoo, or the
late Commander-in-chief of her Majesty's land
forces in New South Wales, trudging it on foot
about his neighbourhood, yet here in Jersey he
may walk about, and dress like any ordinary
mortal, and as if he never had had satraps and

slaves (white and black) to bow down to him in
his life. And you may live as you like, spend
whole days and nights at the club, and play cards,
and have your game of billiards, and no one be
much the wiser for it. Time hangs heavy upon
the hands of these ex-military and naval gentlemen. The club, and parties, and watching for the
arrival of the steamer with the English mails—
these are their only resources. And when these
resources are exhausted, or wearied of, there is
nothing for it but to take to the streets, and to
criticise ladies' dresses and appearances, and to
talk over with some naval or military brother
that last brush with the Sikhs or affair with the
Chinese, and to lament that the business was so
grossly mismanaged, and that the commanding
officer should be obviously so unfit for his duties.

Sir John De Marbury used to meet divers
of these heroes at the club of which he had
been made an honorary member, and it was his
own fault entirely, and not from any lack
of attention on their part, if he was not fully
indoctrinated into all the mysteries of piquet,

and whist, and unlimited loo, and made an expert at billiards and the best mode of "making a canon," as well as put in full possession of the latest intelligence from the seat of war, with a lucid explanation of the various blunders by which it would seem that the British arms were being frequently tarnished in those parts from want of efficient and experienced commanders—like (it was certainly the inference, though not expressed in so many words) the speaker, for instance.

Sir John would come home and amuse his wife, and somewhat shock his mother, by describing club life, and the difficulty experienced by many of the veterans he encountered in the disposing of their time until dinner, and the general weariness and satiety of life under which many were succumbing who had been in their day gallant officers and useful members of society.

At length the day of departure arrived, and Sir John and Lady De Marbury bid farewell to the pleasant isle of Jersey, with its rocky coast, and beautiful bays, and shady lanes, and yonder minarets and crescents glittering in the sun, and to the rugged castle of Elizabeth, with the English flag waving from its hold, guarding the entrance to the harbour.

## CHAPTER XVII.

THE church bells of Donnington are ringing merrily. A flag waves proudly from the old tower. Children are running here and there, with white rosettes pinned to their dresses. The rector and his wife occasionally make their appearance on the scene, and hold hurried consultations with the churchwarden or the schoolmaster or mistress, as it may be. There is eager expectation written upon every countenance: something or other is about to come off. Now one, now another, runs to the top of the hill, whence a good view is obtained of the road leading from the station. At length the distant sound of wheels is heard, as of a carriage rattling over the paved lane which turns off from the main road and leads direct to

Donnington; and now all doubt is dispelled. A
glimpse has been obtained of the postillion's
scarlet jacket as he urges on his horses, and very
soon a close carriage and pair makes its appearance,
and seated in it are the owner of Donnington and
his youthful bride, while in the rumble behind are
Lady De Marbury's maid and Sir John's own man.
The school-children are drawn up in a line, under
the anxious superintendence of the master and
mistress, and forthwith commence singing a song
of welcome which they had been practising the
previous fortnight, but which they, of course, made
a bungle of and sang quite out of tune. Few,
however, noticed it except the master, whose own
composition it was, and set by himself to music:
he had substituted it for the National Anthem,
conceiving it to be, on the whole, a superior
production. There were not, however, half a
dozen there who knew what the children were
singing, or who, if asked the question afterwards,
would have been quite sure that they sang at
all; for there, the moment the carriage draws up
opposite to the church, Mrs. Hulton steps forward

with a splendid bouquet of flowers (*almost* rivalling those of the island Lady De Marbury has but just quitted) and presents it to the bride, who, all smiles, accepts it. The rector then advances and shakes hands with both, and then there are some general inquiries and replies ; and then the singing comes to a close rather abruptly, as it seems, and the churchwarden, as representing the parishioners, comes forward and reads an address of congratulation couched in the most flowery and half-classical style (which could have been the composition of *only* one man in all that group), and then there are the few words of thanks and acknowledgment, and the carriage drives on. Time was, and that not so long ago either, when the natural place of that fair girl in the carriage, who smiled her thanks so graciously to all who approached her, would have been amongst the ranks of those very school-children whom she made such an effort to listen to and comprehend ; and the honest farmer who, with blushing modesty, was endeavouring to get through as well as he could all the fine things " Schoolmeaster Page " had contrived to squeeze into the address, would have considered himself, not to say the equal, but infinitely the superior of her in whose presence it would almost seem as if he was now ready to sink into the earth, so alarmed was he at the sound of his own voice. Such, indeed, is the Cheshire farmer's—we cannot call it exactly respect, and certainly not affection, but his awe and dread of his landlord (he is always haunted by the apprehension of getting " notice to quit " some fine morning, or by receiving a communication from the steward to say that his rent has been raised), that he is quite as much overcome by his feelings of nervousness and apprehension when entering the presence of Squire So-and-so or So-and-so, who are known to be, the one the greatest fool, and the other the hardest drinker in all Cheshire, as he would be if sent for by Lord Powderham or old Squire Legh. Well, the carriage drove on, and the school-children sat down to the treat provided for them in the Rectory grounds; and the master dwelt with pride upon some of his own happily-turned expressions and classical allusions in the address, which, he thinks, *must* have struck Sir John, only that Farmer Thorley read it so badly; and the rector and his wife went about seeing that all the young people were made comfortable; and the bells kept ringing; and so the long-expected day came to a close, and, both at Hall and Rectory, in farm-house and cottage, there was the feeling that all had gone off as it should : the day was fine, the lady and Sir John looked pleased, and the Hall was once more occupied.

It was with feelings of secret wonderment that Lady De Marbury had walked through the ranks of those bowing obsequious domestics as they lined the hall on the day of her arrival at Donnington. The butler looked quite the gentleman, and would probably disdain to sit at table with any of *her* relations. And then the housekeeper—what an awful personage was she, even to glance at, with that curious superstructure of a cap on her head ! She had lived all her life at the Hall, in one capacity or another, and was now getting on towards her threescore years and ten. She must well remember the beginning and rise of Jacob

Delves's fortunes, and whenever they met it would have been, no doubt, as old friends. Indeed, Annie remembered perfectly well her grandfather talking of his friend Mrs. Margaret Evison at the Hall, and being pleased at some token of recollection he had received from her.

And it was the same with others of the old servants and dependents whom she saw as she alighted from the carriage, handed out, as she was, most attentively by her husband, and as she entered her future home. The old gardener, the Scotch steward, the head keeper — gray-headed men all, and who had grown gray in the service of the squires of Donnington — they must all remember old Jacob well, as having been reared at Donnington, and as having laid the foundation of his large fortune in the immediate neighbourhood. Why, they could hardly walk into Newchurch, any of them, now, without stumbling upon some uncle, or aunt, or cousin of hers, any one of whom would deem it an honour to be spoken to by one of the upper servants at the Hall. But not a trace was there to be seen of any such

reminiscences or reflections on a single one of
those many awfully deferential faces she looked
upon : they knew their business too well for that.
In their eyes Lady De Marbury was the representative of twenty, some said thirty, and even
forty thousand pounds, and, true to their instinct,
they fell down and worshipped the golden image.
It was not a feigned, or merely put on for the
occasion, respect on their part, but a thorough,
genuine respect for the owner of so much money.
They were never tired of talking and thinking
about it (as far as such persons are capable of
thinking), and seemed to derive some increased
consequence from talking familiarly to each other
about such large, large sums of money.

Well, Annie was glad enough when the reception was over, and when in the evening, after
dinner and coffee partaken of, she and her
husband were able to shut themselves into the
library, glad to rest from all the fatigues and
excitement of the day. The servants were just
going to their supper, and there was little fear
of their hurrying themselves over *that;* so there

was a good hour before it would be time to summon in the retinue to prayers.

"You look tired, my love," Sir John said
tenderly to his young wife; "and no wonder.
You had better go to bed early, as soon as prayers
are over."

"Oh, I shall be all right, John, presently.
One can't get quite rid of the motion of the
steamer; and then seeing this old place again,
and the church, and all, it rather upsets one."

"Well, my love, I was very happy, at least I
believe I thought so, on the day I came of age;
but it was nothing to what I feel now."

Here we leave it to the experienced reader to
supply for himself, *ad libitum*, any osculatory
details he pleases, by imagining what his own
probable demeanour would have been on such an
occasion.

After, then, any little interruption in the conversation which *may* have taken place—I am
not saying that it did—Sir John went on—

"I remember so well my mother just sitting
where you are now, and my coming in quite

knocked up, having been doing the agreeable the entire day. And we got talking, I recollect, of all the nonsense a poor little fellow called Jones, who was curate here then, had been delivering himself of at the dinner in the tent; and then my mother was crying up that man Marshall and quite swearing by him. How he did take her in, to be sure!"

"She never speaks of him now, I have noticed."

"Ashamed, I suppose."

"Did you like him?"

"Never, until the last; and I didn't like him then. And it wouldn't be true to say I respected him. But I admired his self-devotion, his sacrificing himself in the way he did for the sake of what he believed to be the truth. Mind you, I believe it to be a bad system throughout which would exact such fearful sacrifices from any one, of truth, of honour, of sincerity; but, supposing the system itself was a good one (which of course it isn't), you can't help almost admiring the man who will sacrifice his *all* for it."

"I understand. I remember one of those priests coming to poor grandpapa once."

"It wasn't Delawney, was it—a short, stout, red-faced man?"

"No, it wasn't him. I have seen *him*. No, it was a slight, delicate-looking man."

"Well, what did he want?"

"He said that he had been appointed to the Newchurch 'Mission,' and that, as he heard grandpapa was not bigoted, but a man of a liberal mind and open to conviction, he had come to call upon him."

"Well, what did your grandfather say to that?"

"Oh, he thanked him, and said he was glad to see him. And then the priest went on to regret that there wasn't more love and charity in the world, that there were so many differences about religion, and he said that it was a pity Protestant ministers hated poor Catholics as they did, and told so many stories about them that were not true."

"Well, and how did your grandfather take it all?"

"Oh, grandfather let him go on talking. He was glad to see any one, so that they didn't want money—that is," explained Annie, with a slight blush, "if they didn't come begging for it."

"Well, about the priest?" said Sir John, laughing at her little embarrassment.

"They got on well enough together for some time. But, at last, he began talking about the advantage of being a Catholic, and that for so much money you could procure absolution for your sins, and have masses said for your soul after you were dead, which would be sure to bring you to heaven."

"What did your grandfather say to that?"

"He said he could get his sins forgiven for nothing—without paying any money for it—and he didn't think masses would do any good. The priest wanted to argue with him. But grandfather said, if there was any money to be paid, he would have nothing to do with being a Catholic."

"Did the priest go away then?"

"Yes, he did. And he said if grandfather ever wanted him, to be sure and send for him—that it would be better for him to save his soul than to leave ever so much money behind him to those who would make a bad use of it."

"They are all alike!" said Sir John; and here we drop the curtain, and leave the weary couple to their repose.

# CHAPTER XVIII.

VISITORS, of course, began to pour in apace as soon as Lady De Marbury had made her appearance at church and it was known she was ready to receive them. It is a good neighbourhood all about Newchurch, and there are plenty of carriages and equestrians to be encountered most days on the roads about there. The old woman at the lodge had a busy time of it, what between opening and shutting the gate for visitors. There was a wide-spread curiosity to see how little Annie Delves, as she used to be called by those who were aware of her existence, would comport herself under her new and trying circumstances. Old Squire Legh's report had been highly favourable, when he had returned from his summer outing;

so that people did not go expecting to see anything very *outré* in Sir John's wife. But still
they were not prepared for the perfect composure,
and yet liveliness of manner, which marked Lady
De Marbury's reception of them, and her general
demeanour. As for her beauty, there could not
be a second opinion about *that*. And it was a
kind of beauty connected so much with expression,
and fine dark eyes, and abundance of fair hair,
that it was likely to wear well. Any who had
come with the intention of criticising Annie, and
finding out her defects, had marvellously little to
descant on when they returned home. Anybody
who had come to "patronize" her went away with
the purpose unfulfilled. It was generally allowed
that Sir John could not well have done better.
But how was the difficulty about her poor relations
to be got over? This was the question next raised
for discussion. Would Lady De Marbury acknowledge them? And if she did, what would Sir
John say to it? And then supposing her mother
was to turn up from America, or Australia, or
wherever else it was that she had gone; what was

to be done then ? These were the difficulties to
be faced. People could not have such good luck
without paying dearly for it in some way or other.
Well, these difficulties gave her neighbours a
great deal more concern than they did Lady De
Marbury herself. She was of too truthful and
ingenuous a nature not to have realized her own
position and the duties and responsibilities that
devolved upon her. And she and her husband
had far too much confidence in each other, and
were too sincerely attached, to allow any little
social difficulties that must, under the circumstances, necessarily arise from time to time, to
disturb the good understanding that had from the
first prevailed between them.

"These persons *are* my relations," thought
Lady De Marbury to herself, "and therefore I must not be ashamed to acknowledge
them. It is only by the merest accident in
the world I am not in the same position myself. And every one knows this—all my servants know it—even if I were foolish enough
to try and shut my eyes to it. Then they are

poor, and that is a reason why I, who have so much money at my command, should do something for them. They had as good claims as I had, and, if grandfather had died without a will, they would have been in far different circumstances than they are in now. And, if ignorant and un-cultivated, if I can do nothing for the elders, I can, at any rate, for the children." Thus sensibly did Lady De Marbury put the case to herself, and she was not slow to act upon it. One embarrass-ment, however, she was spared, and for that she *was* thankful. Tom Swigmore, after lounging about Newchurch for some months subsequently to his grandfather's death, had got into a scrape in connection with some farmer's daughter in the neighbourhood; so he had to make a precipitate retreat from the place to avoid the conse-quences, and had gone and enlisted under some feigned name, and had not since been heard of. While giving every weight to the considerations adverted to, and determining, with her husband's sanction, to do her duty towards her relations, Lady De Marbury was not unmindful of what she owed likewise to the man who had honoured her by making her his wife. His rank and position she had been called on to share; she must not, therefore, do anything to tarnish or discredit either. And as there were distinctions of rank all the world over, and as it was necessary to keep up those distinctions, Lady De Marbury came to the conclusion that she would best discharge her duty, not by indiscriminate visiting amongst her relations, but by pensioning the aged and infirm among them, by setting the sons up in business, portioning the daughters, and paying for the education of the children. And all this, which was one of her first cares after getting settled at Donnington, she was enabled to do both to her husband's and her own satisfaction, and principally through the ready instrumentality of Mr. Hulton, their rector. The aged and sick among them she visited with regularity. Nor did she ever, in any instance, experience annoyance or embarrassment from any inopportune or over-eager claiming of relationship amongst her kindred. Such was the happy result of recognising the natural claims

of relationship without being betrayed into a
disregard of the feelings of those with whom she
had become allied.

It has been mentioned already that Annie's
mother had married a second time and settled in
America.   No tidings had been heard of her since
that time, though she had been written to by her
daughter immediately after the death of her grandfather.   It was not known whether she was alive.
The two or three letters that had been written had
never come back; so it might be presumed that
*some one* had received them—some one of her
family, if not herself.   It was understood that she
had intended to settle in Mobile, but nothing more
was known about her; and so things remained for
several months after the arrival of Sir John and
Lady De Marbury at the Hall.   But one afternoon—it was in the early part of January—Lady
De Marbury was informed that some one wished
to see her on particular business.   "He is a
respectable-looking man," the servant said, and
had been shown into the housekeeper's room.
Upon repairing thither, a middle-aged man,

dressed in black, and who appeared to be in
the rank of a tradesman, or, perhaps, small farmer,
rose up to greet her. He was a sad-looking
person, but intelligent, and had with him two
little boys of about the ages of nine and six
respectively. They were slight, fair-haired children, with fresh complexions and bright faces, but
did not look strong : they bore no resemblance to
the person who brought them, he being dark and
sallow. The little boys looked up wistfully at the
pleasant face of the lady as she entered the room ;
and her heart seemed to yearn towards them,
though she knew not, as yet, their sad history ; for
sad it must be, she thought, from the little attempt
at mourning about their dresses that at once
struck her eye. The black ribbon which confined
their shirt-collars, and the little bit of crape about
their caps, both told of some recent bereavement.

"Lady De Marbury," said the man respectfully,
"my name is Johnson. I have come many thousand miles to see you, and to fulfil the dying
request of the parents of these two little helpless
orphan children. I have brought them all the

way from Mobile, in the Southern States of America. They are the children—the only ones left—of your mother, Mary Venables." Thus far did the man proceed, when Lady De Marbury, bursting into tears, drew towards her those mother-less and fatherless children and gave way for a long time to successive bursts of grief. She had felt, from the moment she saw them, an instinctive going forth of her heart towards them; and now, as she looked upon their little innocent, uncon-scious faces, they wondering at the great lady's tears—for, poor things, they had well-nigh for-gotten all the sad events of the past few months—she could not, for some time, control her emotion. Making an effort, however, to restrain her feelings, she intimated to her visitor that he should proceed.

"It has been a sad case, and I would have you, Lady De Marbury, ask for strength from on high to hear what more I have to tell you. I keep a store myself in a little village called Winchester, in Mobile State. I have lived there several years, though I am a native of this country. It is a most unhealthy place and sur-

rounded with swamps. However, I have got used
to it, and, praised be the Lord! have prospered
there, though I have had several bad fevers and
sharp attacks of ague. Mine is well-nigh the
only store there, and I deal in everything, I may
say. I do all the undertaker's business for fifty
miles round, and that alone would keep a man in
constant employ. On Sundays, also, I preach, as
there is no parson or place of worship within a
hundred miles. It is about two years ago, come
next Lady Day, since Thomas Venables and his
wife fixed themselves in a location near to Winchester. He had bought a deal of marshy land
from one of these agents up the country, and
thought to drain it and to make it into pasture
and tillage. He had never seen the place, and I
reckon he had gotten it cheap; but he never did
rightly tell me what he gave for it. Well, ma'am,
when they came to Winchester they were as
healthy a looking family as you would wish to see
—quite old-countrylike-looking folk. He had
been a Cheshire farmer in a small way, I reckon,
somewhere near Northwich; and the missus, she

was fine and clever too when she came, and with *such* a spirit! 'Only let master,' she would say to me when she came into my store to get any little thing, 'put a few tiles in, and drain that land he has taken, and see if I don't turn you out as fine a cheese as they'd make in Cheshire.' But I knew better than that. However, as I was saying, they were as healthy a looking family as you would wish to see, considering especially they had been some years out in America, in the Northern States somewhere. When they came to Winchester they had four children—a girl, the eldest, about eight or nine, these two, and a baby in arms. Well, ma'am, not to make too long a story of it, the master, he did work, might and main, at that land of his, striving to drain it and to bring it under cultivation, and to make pasturage for a few cows; and I *do* believe that he would have succeeded, after all, in making something of the land, but that he was pulled down, first by rheumatic fever, then by a long attack of ague, which kept him to his bed ten weeks together, and when he got up he was fit for nothing. And then the missus, she did strive and strive till she nearly killed herself. 'We don't like, Mr. Johnson,' she would say to me, 'to throw all our money and labour away; but, if we can only realize something by the sale of this land, and get away with our lives—for it be a dreadfully unhealthy place— we shall be only too thankful.' But, poor dear ! she never *did* get away from it alive. First one, then another of the children was taken bad. The youngest of these two had it worse than any of them, and no one thought he would ever get over it. It was some kind of low fever, the doctor said. The eldest girl died first, then the baby ; after that the master sickened and was soon gone. The missus bore up bravely to the last : she was so busy nursing these two little ones that it seemed almost as if she had not time to be ill. No one thought this young one would recover ; but at length the doctor said he might pull through ; and it was only then that missus gave way. She had overtaxed her strength, I take it ; for, from the very first, after she was taken ill, she gave herself up and said she should never recover. So one night late she sends for me. 'Mr. Johnson,' she said, 'I feel that I am not long for this world. The only thing that troubles me is about those two dear children sleeping in their cribs there. If I thought they'd be taken care of, I could be well content to follow my husband and my other two children. I have a daughter in England, who would be married by this time and who is well off. Take those two children to her, and charge her, as her mother's last dying request, never to let them want—never to forget that they are her brothers, and, as she hopes to meet her own mother in heaven, to be herself a tender careful mother to these poor dear little boys whom I am leaving behind me.' She then charged me to place in your hands this parcel, containing a locket of your own hair, which she had brought with her from England, with a few other things, and also told me to make what I could of their house and the things in it, and to sell the land, when I could with advantage, and to let the money be for the benefit of these two children and to pay for the expenses of removing them to England."

Her visitor then placed in Lady De Marbury's hands a small brown-paper parcel, which, from the hasty glance she took at it, seemed to contain a few trifling ornaments, including the locket referred to, a Bible and Prayer Book, with the name "Mary Eckersley, Newchurch," written in both. There were also three or four letters, written in a school-girl's hand, which Lady De Marbury had no difficulty in recognising as having been addressed by herself to her mother after she had gone to America.

"Did my mother ever say anything," asked Lady De Marbury, her voice broken with sobs, "about those letters I wrote her, and why they remained unanswered? Did she ever speak of writing to me?"

"I reckon," replied Johnson, with a little hesitation, "that missus wasn't much of a scholar, nor master either, for the matter of that; but she did say, many a time and oft, sure enough, that she would get me to write a letter for her to her daughter in England, when she knew for certain that she was married and returned from abroad.

R

She had been told that the old madam had carried
you off to a distance, somewhere, and I reckon she
thought it was no use writing to you until you
were your own mistress, like.    You will excuse me,
my lady, for making so free?"

"There is not the least occasion for apology,"
replied Lady De Marbury, with sweetness. "I
thank you from my heart for having brought
these two dear children to me.   They are my
brothers, and as my brothers they shall be treated.
I accept my dear, dearest mother's parting charge.
These children shall be reared as tenderly as if
they were my own : they shall be properly educated
and put out in life.   I can answer for my husband
as I can for myself.   And now, Mr. Johnson, I
must commit you and these two dear children to
the care of my housekeeper, for the present, while
I go and find Sir John, and communicate to him
all the painful intelligence of which you have been
the bearer, and inform him of the important
charge I am about to take on me.   My housekeeper
will supply you and these little fellows with any
refreshment you may require."

Saying this, and tenderly kissing her little brothers, she went out of the room to find her husband. Sir John was standing, in conversation
with one of the keepers, at a little distance from
the house, when he was joined by his wife.

"Let us take a turn in the shrubberies, dear,"
she said, taking his arm. "I have heard something that has greatly agitated and distressed
me."

"Nothing about my mother, is it?"

"No; nothing about *your* mother, but about
mine. Oh, John! my dearest mother is dead: I
have just heard it;" and she leaned upon her
husband's shoulder, and wept bitterly for some
time.

"My darling, I will try and make up to you for
every loss by double tenderness and affection. Do
not, dearest Annie, give way to such grief. Come
and sit down in this arbour, and tell me what you
have heard, and who told you."

"There is a man here who has come all the way
from Mobile in the Southern States, and who has
been giving me such a sad account of all the sick-

ness and sufferings that befell my dearest mother and the whole family. First, two of the children died from some kind of low fever, then the father, and last of all, quite worn out by sorrow and suffering, my own dearest mother; and oh, John, she has left me, as a charge, as a parting legacy, and with her dying breath, two of the sweetest children— little boys—I have ever seen! Oh, it is heart-rending to see their little innocent faces, and how unconscious they seem of the great loss they have sustained! I have promised, John, to receive them as a sacred charge from my dying mother, always to care for them as if they were my own, and to be their friend and a mother to them as long as I live. Have I your sanction?"

"My best beloved," said her husband, tenderly embracing her, "you can never do anything wrong as long as you follow the dictates of your own loving heart. You have never disappointed me yet. You have been throughout most kind, and yet judicious, in all you have done for your relations. We will go and see these poor little fellows you speak of, and, whatever you settle about the matter, you may depend upon my concurrence."

When they returned to the house, and sought out the housekeeper's room, they found Mr. Johnson, who had partaken of some refreshment, engaged with a newspaper which happened to be in the room, while the two little boys had opened the window and were playing quietly together in a little garden that was outside. From his visitor Sir John heard what was pretty much a repetition of his wife's narrative to him in the shrubbery, with enlargements; while Lady De Marbury, stepping out through the window, carried off the little boys to show them the pigeons and other objects of interest and curiosity to them.

Mr. Johnson took his departure in due time, and shortly afterwards returned to America, where, by the last accounts, he was doing an extensive business at Winchester, Mobile State, as an undertaker and general merchant. The little boys remained under their sister's special charge until she considered them old enough and strong enough to be sent as week-day boarders to the Grammar School in Newchurch; and on every Saturday, as a general thing, and when it was fine enough, Lady De Marbury was to be seen driving her pair of ponies into Newchurch to bring out Harry and Arthur to the Hall until the Monday. This was the pleasantest occupation of the week to her; and as she saw the glow of health returning into the once delicate countenances of her little brothers, and heard their ringing laugh as they played about the orchards and shrubberies of Donnington, she felt how much "more blessed it is to give than to receive," and that (with the exception of the gift of a fond and devoted husband) no pleasure or advantage which she had derived from her grandfather's will at all came up to the delight of tenderly caring for those two fatherless and motherless little boys.

## CHAPTER XIX.

WE left the Dowager Lady De Marbury, as she is now entitled to be called, in Jersey, and there she remained until the period for which her house was taken had expired. And this was at the Michaelmas succeeding the departure of her son and daughter. She then bid adieu, in all probability for ever, to that pleasant island, and looked for the last time upon the wide-spreading chestnuts whose leaves were beginning to turn and drop off, and the vine-covered house, with the grapes fast ripening under so genial a sun, and her garden of flowers where she and Annie had spent so many quiet happy days, and upon all those little nameless things about a place to which we get so accustomed, and which the

eye rests upon with gladness, morning after
morning, when we come forth and breathe the
fresh air of heaven. At no period of the year,
indeed, does Jersey appear to more advantage
than in the autumn, when the heat of summer
has passed away and the golden fruit hangs ripe
in many an orchard. Large clusters of grapes
are gathered by the peasants, and eaten in homely
fashion along with their bread; and their minia-
ture harvest is being gathered in, each little spot
of ground growing that which, with frugality, will
supply the family's wants until another twelve-
month comes round.

After a certain period of life most persons dislike change, not in the abstract so much, but
when it comes to be carried out. If we have
stayed at a place, even for a few weeks or months,
when we come to leave it (unless we are more
than ordinarily unfortunate) we do so with reluctance. For we have got to be familiar with
its land-marks, and to take some interest in its
local politics and feuds. We may never see the
place again, and possibly our sojourn there has

had a character of its own stamped upon it—
joyous, or the reverse—by occurrences which have
interrupted the even tenour of our lives, and which
cause us ever afterwards to associate them with
some of the inanimate objects which surrounded
us at the time. Thoughts such as these thronged
through Lady De Marbury's mind as she drove
through the quiet streets of St. Hélier, just beginning to awake into fresh life, and proceeded along
the pier on her way to the steamer. There was
the usual miscellaneous assemblage which marks
the departure of the steamer everywhere. Cabs
driving hastily up and discharging themselves of
their fare; and then what piles of boxes and
portmanteaus come off the roof, and are thrown
one on top of the other upon the ground, immediately to be seized upon by three or four men,
each with a little brass plate, having a number on
it, on his arm, and conveyed off by him you know
not where, except that he seems to go in the
direction where the steamer is puffing and its
smoke blending with the morning air.

Then there are the groups of friends come down

thus early to see some member of the family off, and the tender farewells, and promises to write. Then there is the single man who has nobody to care for him, and whose only luggage is a portmanteau and hat-box, besides the plaid and umbrella which he prefers carrying himself. To him all these adieus, and promises to write, and this wiping of eyes, seem supremely ludicrous, and he is half tempted to express his sentiments on the subject to that pretty-looking girl who keeps waving her handkerchief to the group on the pier, and wiping her eyes, by turns. There is a great bustle now. A spring cart, driven by a man in a red-laced coat, with a gold band round his hat, comes tearing along the pier, scattering people right and left, and clearing the way up to where the steamer is lying. These are the mails. Great leathern bags, and a sack or two, are pitched upon the ground, immediately seized on, and hurried on board. The ladder is withdrawn, bells ring in quick succession, a crisis is evidently imminent, handkerchiefs now are waved with redoubled energy, the steam is up,

the vessel has a slight motion about it, when a
cab is descried by some half-dozen porters all at
once, driving at full speed along the pier, loaded
with luggage. It is just half an hour after the
time. The captain from his elevation on the
paddle-box fumes, and frets, and utters curses,
as the ladder is thrown across again, and a whole
heap of luggage finds its way on board on the
backs of sturdy porters. The owner comes last,
taking everything very quietly, and apparently
not at all crediting that the steamer was actually
going so soon as the choleric captain would have
him believe. However, there is no mistake this
time. "Now then, go ahead!" the captain shouts
out; and soon the vessel is steaming out of the
harbour, and the people on the pier are reduced
to a mere speck, and the weeping girl puts by her
pocket-handkerchief and takes to smelling and
admiring her bouquet. And the single gentleman
pays her some attention, and offers her the use
of his plaid, and so she is "comforted." All
subside into their places presently, for there is
usually a swell between Jersey and Guernsey;

and so the steamer ploughs its watery way to Southampton.

Lady De Marbury had taken everything very quietly from the first, as she well might, with her own maid and man-servant to look after things and see them on board; and then she had settled herself quietly upon the deck, with an awning over her, and spent the time very tranquilly with her book and knitting until they had passed the Isle of Wight and found themselves steaming up the river. Apartments at " Radley's " had been engaged for her, and here she rested for the night.

Next day she left for Bath, and in the course of the afternoon was once more installed in her own house in the Crescent, which had been let during her absence. At Bath Lady De Marbury was at home, and knew most of the clergy, and the resident families of any note. She mixed principally, indeed almost exclusively, with those who constituted the " serious society " of the place. As the clergy, without any exception, belonged to that peculiar section of the Church denominated

"Evangelical," and of which Lady De Marbury (as became her father's daughter) had been at all times a stanch adherent, it was natural that she should cultivate their acquaintance and that of their families, and that her house should be at all times hospitably thrown open to them. As everybody knows, there is no end of private and proprietary chapels in Bath, with all sorts of fantastic names—the Laura, the Octagon, and so on —each maintaining its own pet parson, and in a state of glorious independence of the parish church, or any other church. Well, the chapel that Lady De Marbury patronized was the Pentagon (you will not find it in the "Clergy List"). She had preferred it above all its rivals, by reason of the superior "gifts" and deeper spiritual experience of its incumbent, the Rev. Henry O'Neil (half of the popular, and one or two of the unpopular as well, preachers in Bath are Irish) which she conceived him to be the possessor of above all his brethren in that city. Well, in her absence this Mr. O'Neil had had a "call," or whatever they phrase it, to a proprietary chapel in London, which

had the advantage of having a much handsomer
income attached to it than the Pentagon, though
that was not despicable as clerical incomes go.
And this "call" Mr. O'Neil had "seen his way"
to accept. So that, when Lady De Marbury returned to Bath, she found a successor installed in
Mr. O'Neil's place. There had been great competi-
tion for the appointment, and each of the candidates
had preached before a select committee of trustees
and pew-holders, both male and female, and the
election had fallen upon a countryman and personal
friend of the late incumbent, one Mr. Mahon.
Now it never once occurred to Lady De Marbury
that she could have had any previous acquaintance
with this Mr. Mahon. She hardly troubled herself
about the clergyman's name. It was of no sort of
importance to her what it was or where he came
from. The one great point with her was, was
he a "faithful minister?" Did he preach the
Gospel? and was it in a "searching way?" If
these questions could be answered satisfactorily,
she did not really care who he was. It was not
the man, but the minister she thought of. When,

therefore, she heard the ladies of her acquaintance, one and all, raving about their new minister, panegyrizing his appearance, quoting his beautiful metaphors, and dwelling upon the unction of his extempore addresses, she was all anxiety to go and hear him. This she could not do for a Sunday or two after her arrival in Bath, on account of illness; but at length she was able to get out, and the very first walk she took (contrary, by the way, to the advice of her medical man) was to church—to the Pentagon, where she prepared herself for a rich spiritual treat. The place was crowded, galleries and all. And at length the "clerical Adonis" (as he was nicknamed by those who were jealous of him, or who were carnally-minded) made his appearance. He was a tall, stout, handsome man, with fine black whiskers, and hair of the same colour, well brushed, and with a division down the centre of it. His voice, for such a great, big, stout man, was low and rather mincing. He made a long extempore prayer before the sermon which abounded in Scripture phrases, and then threw himself into the sermon with an energy and a

zest which proved pretty plainly that he knew
what was expected of him; that if he didn't please
the critical audience, and rows of Evangelical
ladies before him, he might as well go about his
business. And never, it was admitted, during the
few months he had been there, had Mr. Mahon
acquitted himself more satisfactorily than he had
done upon this occasion. His auditors seemed to
hang upon his every word; and as soon as church
was over, and the congregation dismissed, such
words as "How beautiful!" "What a dear man!"
"What a sweet preacher!" echoed on every side.
Lady De Marbury had not listened to him in the
pulpit five minutes before she recognised in Mr.
Mahon her quondam chaplain and admirer. She
had a better view of him when he ascended the
pulpit than in the reading-desk, and his identity
flashed upon her in an instant, though it must
have been a good dozen years and upwards since
she had seen him. That he was aware who formed
one of his hearers could admit of little doubt, both
from the unusual eloquence and fervour he had exhibited, which had struck several, and also because

Lady De Marbury was a person of too much importance in the religious world of Bath for her name not to have reached the ears of Mr. Mahon (he had dropped the Mac), or for the circumstance of her being an attendant at the Pentagon not to be well known to him.

It was some consolation to know that he was married. He had married a rich widow in Bath, some years older than himself, when, a short time previously to his appointment, he had been taking duty in the neighbourhood. It was a puzzle to Lady De Marbury to know what it was best to do. To leave the chapel without assigning any reason would give rise to comment, and would no doubt be construed by her "religious friends" into disapproval of the object of their enthusiastic praise; while to assign *the* reason was not to be thought of. There would be something ludicrous in associating her name—who was now a grave, staid, matronly-looking person—with that of a young handsome man like Mr. Mahon. No; the less said about it the better. She would meet him, as she would have to meet him some

time or other, as a mere casual acquaintance. It was not probable that *he* would allude
to the past, and it was quite certain that she
would not. She felt, however, for the awkward-
ness he must experience at seeing one who had
all but turned him out of her house, and who had
dismissed him with less ceremony than she would
have used towards her butler. She would therefore assume a gracious demeanour, and be the first
to show that she wished by-gones to be by-gones.
She need not, however, have made herself uneasy.
Mr. Mahon, the popular preacher of Bath, and the
indispensable ornament at so many tea-tables, was
a very different person from her former chaplain,
running over with drollery, and an adept at all
athletic sports.

She encountered him and his wife unexpectedly
at a house in the Crescent, where she went to pay
a morning call. Her first impulse was to advance
and shake hands with him; but, perceiving no
tokens of recognition on his part, she returned his
ceremonious bow in a similar fashion. The tone he
adopted was that of exalted spirituality; and if he

condescended to take part in any merely secular conversation, it was under protest, as it were. One or two of Lady De Marbury's remarks upon some common-place subject of the day he took up, and, speaking in his capacity of spiritual adviser of the assembled party, appeared slightly to take exception to, as savouring too much of the earth, earthy. He spoke in very low tones, and with unctuousness of manner; but there was no mistaking his meaning: he considered Lady De Marbury's remarks as lacking spirituality, as savouring too much of the things of time.

His wife, who was a showily-dressed, rather fine-looking woman, though her features were plain, and who talked a great deal, slightly patronized Lady De Marbury, and evidently looked upon her as one who had been formerly the victim of a misplaced passion, slightly reprehensible, under all the circumstances, and considering the disparity of years between the parties; she therefore "adopted a tone" as much as to say, "You see *I* am in the place that you once wished to occupy. It was natural, no doubt, upon your part.

But the thing is now hopeless." Altogether, Lady De Marbury felt rather put out. "For *him* to be giving me a lecture, indeed! *She* to adopt that tone of superiority and pity!" And it must be admitted that it was rather mortifying to Lady De Marbury to be treated so—that he should be monopolizing the conversation to a certain extent, and then, when his wife did speak, that she should do nothing but quote her husband's authority and appeal to him. "What account," she thought to herself as she walked slowly back to her house, "can he have given his wife of his former life at Donnington Hall, that she should so plainly presume upon it?"

## CHAPTER XX.

It is a long time since we have heard anything of the Rev. Father Delawney. It will be recollected that he did not come very well out of that affair of Mr. Marshall's. The suspicion of being an accomplice hung over him. It was in vain for him to deprecate the uncharitable surmises which he said Protestants were so ready to entertain against "poor Catholics." It was not by any means an easy matter to put the Rev. Father out of countenance. Almost the only time he was ever known to falter, and look a little abashed, was when Sir John questioned him closely, in the presence of some of the farmers, as to his knowledge all along of Mr. Marshall's real character. The hesitation was certainly but for a moment;

and it may possibly have been the case, as he said it was, that he was too much hurt and surprised at such questions being put to him to be able to make an immediate answer. And he seemed rather to dwell upon the indignity that had been put upon him, and upon people's willingness to believe the worst wherever a priest was concerned, than to be in any hurry to answer the questions that were put to him. However, he was understood to deny the charge in general terms; that is, he said that "of course if he had known for certain that Mr. Marshall was a Jesuit, it would have been his duty to have informed Sir John." But even this was not quite satisfactory. For, as Mr. Hulton said, how few can be said to know *for certain* what another is, however conclusive the evidence; and then, though it might certainly have been his *duty* to have disclosed what he knew, yet the performance of a duty is often postponed for what are alleged to be sufficient reasons. Who is to be the judge of those reasons? The priest might have thought that there were sufficient reasons for postponing the performance of his duty until Sir John had become a Catholic, until Mr. Marshall had left—in a word, might have postponed it *sine die.* Who can tell? Altogether, as far as the Father was concerned, people were not one bit the wiser than they were before. The priest assumed the air of injured innocence, and was looked upon by his flock as the victim of Protestant intolerance and malevolence.

It was not very easy to know what to do. Father Delawney had been so long an appendage to Donnington that Sir John was unwilling to resort to any harsh and discourteous steps, such as his mother, and (it must be admitted) the rector too, urged upon him. He was allowed, therefore, to go on his old way; only he was never invited afterwards to sit down to table at the Hall. All this was immediately subsequent to the discovery of Mr. Marshall's real character. But about the period of Sir John's marriage a rumour reached him that Father Delawney had expressed himself as actuated by a strong desire to seek the chair of St. Peter and throw himself

at the feet of the Holy Father. This was a very
welcome piece of intelligence to Sir John and to
the other ruling powers at Donnington. And
most fervently did they hope that nothing would
occur to prevent the Rev. Father from carrying
out such a pious design. Sir John had at the
time things of more importance to think about;
but after the stir connected with his marriage
was over, and the necessary legal business consequent upon that event had been got through, he
had leisure to make inquiries respecting the Rev.
Father's intentions. Great was his delight then
to hear that Priest Delawney was not only thinking of going to Rome, but that he had actually
gone, and was to be absent two years. Donnington was to be served by the priest who had
been recently appointed to the Newchurch Mission,
the same reverend gentleman who undertook to
make poor old Jacob Delves easy about his sins
for a pecuniary consideration.

"Now is the time to do something," thought
Sir John. He could not pull down the Roman
Catholic chapel without the consent of the Vicar-

Apostolic of the district, who resided at Birmingham. But the house the priest lived in belonged to Sir John, and could be resumed by him at pleasure, upon giving due notice. This, however, was only to be resorted to as a *dernier*.

An amicable negotiation was at once set on foot with the proper authorities, whereby Sir John undertook, on condition of being allowed to level to the ground the old chapel by the mere, to contribute a certain sum towards the erection of a chapel in Newchurch (where it was really wanted), and to provide the priest there with a house rent free. This was carried out after a lengthened negotiation. At times it seemed as if nothing would come of it; there were so many permissions to be asked, and dispensations granted, and conditions acceded to. One of these written conditions was that "no Protestant" (it was wished to insert the words "or heretical," but Sir John objected) "place of worship should be erected upon the now site, or within five hundred yards of the now site, of the

Chapel of St. Thomas of Canterbury, Martyr and Confessor, at Donnington, and that none of the stones, nor any part of the present building, be applied, under any circumstances whatever, to the erection of any such Protestant place of worship."

Sir John had, at length, the satisfaction of seeing the place fairly dismantled. He gave permission to the late owners to carry away everything that could be of service to them in building their new chapel. And this having been done, and the walls being left standing, with the remains of the east window and the doorway, he turned it into the present very picturesque ruin, covered with ivy, which any one may see for himself who makes an expedition to Donnington, and can find his way to the place.

Thus was rooted up, at last, and effectually, a Romish settlement which had existed at Donnington ever since the reign of Edward I., and with it seem to have disappeared all hopes and expectations of winning back the heir of the De Marburys to the ancient faith. It was said at the time, but I know not with what truth, that, after considering the matter for two years, the Sacred Congregation at Rome pronounced judgment in the case of the Donnington Mission, and condemned Fathers Paul and Delawney as having been guilty of "indiscretion," and admonished them as to their future carriage.

There is some reason to believe that Father Delawney's journey to Rome was not quite as voluntary a one as he wished people to believe, but that it was the result of a peremptory summons from the Sacred Congregation to enable them to arrive at a definite conclusion. As for the stories that were in circulation as to the Rev. Father's having fallen into the hands of the Most Holy Inquisition, they may be dismissed, I think, as fabulous; the fact being that he was allowed to take up his residence at the English College, where he ended his days several years afterwards.

A remedy had now been applied to one standing source of annoyance, and, as it had proved upon more than one occasion, of serious mischief. The proselytizing zeal of the Romish clergy found

ample scope amongst the smaller tradespeople of
Newchurch, and even succeeded in winning over,
to the outward profession of religion, at any rate,
two or three hoary-headed reprobates, who had
long been proof against the warnings and exhortations of their own ministers.  But Sir John De
Marbury and his family were henceforth left in
peace, and he was no longer regarded in the light
of one who had eluded indeed for a time the loving
vigilance of his holy mother the Church, but
who would be sure, be it sooner or be it later, to
seek a reconciliation with her, and be numbered
amongst the sheep of her fold.

Another eyesore yet remained to be dealt
with, though of a minor description; and that
was to get rid of the ugly meeting-house-
style of building which had so long disfigured
the park.  The matter had been often talked
over between Sir John and his wife as a thing
that it would be desirable to accomplish at the
first favourable opportunity, and that opportunity
was not long in presenting itself.  Lady De
Marbury had found herself, after being put in pos-

session of her fortune, richer, by several thousand pounds, than she had expected. Some money that had been long looked upon as lost, and which had been lent out at high interest by her grandfather several years previously to his death, had been unexpectedly repaid with interest and compound interest; and this sum, amounting in all to five or six thousand pounds, Lady De Marbury resolved to devote to the building of a memorial church to her grandfather. Plans and specifications were soon fixed upon, and in due time a small, elegant-looking church, with tapering spire, took the place of that ugly red-brick structure, with its staring windows, which always had seemed to bear, in its unlovely features, traces of its schismatical origin, and of the many painful incidents connected with its history from the very first.

It was a pleasant day, and a day to be thankful for, when the white-robed procession of choristers and clergy, chanting psalms, wended their way across the park from the school-house, and entered those about-to-be-consecrated portals.

For here at the entrance they were joined by
the Bishop of the Diocese, who at once commenced the office of consecration—walking up
the nave towards the spacious chancel amidst
a throng of worshippers on either side of him.
The petition for consecration was presented
by Sir John, and the usual services performed,
with a sermon by the bishop, and the whole was
appropriately concluded with the Holy Communion.  No pains or expense had been spared
to make this little church, with its open seats and
encaustic tiles, in some degree worthy of the high
and holy purpose to which it was to be henceforth
exclusively devoted.  Most of the windows were
filled with stained glass of exquisite beauty.  But
the one which attracted the greatest share of attention, and the effect of which was most striking as
you entered the church on the south side, was the
memorial window erected by his grand-daughter
and her husband to Jacob Delves.  It was a beautiful representation of the Resurrection, with the
inscription at foot, "In memoriam Jacobi Delves,
de Newchurch, qui obiit sext. die Septembris, A.D.

mdcccxliii., ætate lxxxiii. Jesu merci." And a handsome brass plate, which had been let into the wall upon one side of the window, contained this inscription, in Old English letters of red and black: "This window has been erected by John De Marbury, of Donnington, in the county of Chester, Baronet, and Dame Annie his wife, in memory of Jacob Delves, formerly of Donnington, and who was grandfather of the aforesaid Dame Annie De Marbury. He endowed this parish with £200 for the benefit of the poor for ever. 'Ye have the poor with you always, and whensoever ye will ye may do them good.' (S. Mark xiv. 7)."

It was with streaming eyes that Annie, after the services of the day were all over and her guests had departed, stole down to this beautiful church again, all quiet now, and with its holy character yet fresh upon it, and prostrated herself before its altar in humble recognition of that "goodness and mercy which had followed her all the days of her life." She was overcome with thoughts of the past, —with the remembrance of the first time she had ever seen her husband, and her awe of him—with

the recollection of the solemn scene by her grandfather's death-bed, he just waiting to see his
fondest wish fulfilled before his soul should wing
its flight to the everlasting habitations of the just;
and then all her varied life since, and the strange
places and scenes she had visited. But most
touching of all were the thoughts of her dead
mother, and of the cup of bitterness that had been
given her to drink to the very dregs, dying in
a distant land, and bequeathing those helpless
orphans to her daughter's care and tender pity.
Well, she would, with God's help, strive and do
her duty by them. Her mother was, alas! gone
beyond her reach before she could receive any
tokens of a daughter's love. But these children!
she thanked God she had an opportunity of
showing her regard for her mother's memory by
the care she took of them. And then thoughts of
the day's religious services came into her mind—
all so soothing and fraught with blessing. Here
they had been enabled to build a house in some
degree worthy of that Being to whose worship it
was now solemnly dedicated; and the comfort it

was to think that daily prayers would now be henceforward offered up in this beautiful church. Mr. Hulton had gladly promised this, and to provide for the duty, both on Sundays and week-days, until some more permanent arrangement could be made.

Annie was yet kneeling before the altar, ab-sorbed in grateful recollection of past mercies, and in forming good resolutions for the future, when the faintest, gentlest breathing by her side attracted her notice and roused her from her contemplation.

First one of her little brothers, and then the other, she perceived standing close by her, as if they would associate themselves with her in the solemn religious exercise they found her engaged in; and, in a moment afterwards, her husband, who had been seeking her, and who, with the little boys, had entered the sacred build-ing so noiselessly as not to have attracted his wife's notice, approached, and silently took his place beside her. They remained thus devoutly employed for several minutes, and with the two

T

children kneeling likewise. Afterwards they rose up, with a fresh bond of union, as it were, between them, and, with tranquil joy in their hearts, returned to the house.

## CHAPTER XXI.

WE left the Dowager Lady De Marbury a little ruffled at the almost contemptuous way in which her advances had been met by the now popular minister of the Pentagon and his not very refined wife. It really seemed as if they were determined to be beforehand in the exhibition of indifference, if not hostility.

The reverend gentleman, it may be presumed, was fully alive to the advantage of being the first to gain possession of the public ear. Though it does not ensure your triumph, yet, undoubtedly, it conduces to it. Many will not be at the trouble of contradicting injurious reports, however false or exaggerated they be ; many go about it un- skilfully, and damage their own cause by intem-

perance of language or the rashness of their proceedings; and some there are who succumb at
once, lose heart, and turn their backs upon the
enemy.

To one, then, whose bread depended in some
measure upon his popularity, and to whom the
applause of his listeners, and the admiration of
men generally, were as the breath of his nostrils
(though he counted such things, he often said, as
mere vanity), it was obviously of importance to
anticipate any hostile movement, or even any
disclosures affecting his reputation, which might
emanate from Lady De Marbury. Mr. Mahon
knew enough of the world to be aware that, situated
as he was, any whispers of former indiscretion or
levity of behaviour, upon his part, would weaken
the hold he had over his flock far more effectually
than any display of avowed enmity.

A popular preacher's position is eminently a fac-
titious one. He is not really any wiser, or better,
or more sensible than the generality of his brethren,
frequently the reverse. But the two things in his
favour, and which are his entire stock-in-trade, are,

first, that a certain number of people have agreed to think that *he is* a superior being, and have staked their credit to that effect; and, secondly, that he has the tact and skill to keep up that impression amongst the members of his flock. But once shake his people's faith in him, and down comes the whole structure in a run. To men of the world there may seem to be something almost contemptible in a great big fellow like Mahon always speaking (especially to ladies) in that low unctuous tone, so as scarcely to be heard a yard off; and they ask why he should take people's hands in that tender, affectionate way, and hold them in his so long, and then take his leave with that fervent clasp; and whether it is absolutely necessary that, amongst the elderly portion of his flock, the popular preacher's conversation should be so exclusively upon religious topics.

But people who cavil in this way have never fairly realized to themselves the necessities of the popular preacher's position. If he were to speak and act like other people, his prestige would at once vanish. The female mind needs sympathy: it must be addressed in soothing, gentle phraseology.

If he, therefore, *does* take the single lady's hand
and press it, and look into her eyes, and murmur
a few words of inquiry, or condolence, or what not,
where is the harm ?  *She* likes to be thus accosted,
and practice has made it easy for *him*.  So they
are *both* satisfied.  Why shouldn't we be ?

A little mild persecution never comes amiss to the
popular preacher, especially if his persecutor be an
episcopal one.  It makes him at once an object of
sympathy, even with those to whom he was before
one of indifference.  Delicate health, domestic
troubles, the reputation of holding " startling
views "—such as that the world is coming to an end
in the course of a year or two, that the Millennium
is at hand—may all be turned to account by one who
knows his business.  These things keep up people's
interest in him, make him the subject of general
conversation.  But anything calculated to strip
him of his pretensions, to make him appear as a
charlatan and adventurer, to throw ridicule upon
his antecedents — these are things to be most
carefully guarded against if you wish to retain
your place.  For who would value the attentions

of a man who had been almost "turned off" for his presumption in making love to his mistress? And then to think of the present popular preacher of the Pentagon being the same as the love-stricken spouter of Moore and Byron a few years back! Is it certain that he is so very much changed?

It will be admitted, therefore, that Mr. Mahon showed common sense in this instance, at any rate, when he decided upon the part he should act. What he told his wife we have no means of knowing; but I much fear that, if it was the truth, it was not "the whole truth, and nothing but the truth." For how could she have got it into her head that, in years gone by, this very Lady De Marbury, meek and saint-like though she looked now, had made advances to her son's tutor and her own chaplain, and that, if Mr. Mahon was not now the husband of this lady, it was his own fault, and not hers? How could such an idea have got into Mrs. Mahon's head? It can only, I think, admit of one explanation, and that is, that she derived her information from her husband himself. Be that as it may, Mrs. Mahon's demeanour

towards her was very far indeed from being
agreeable to Lady De Marbury. It said, as
plainly as words could say, "How mortified you
must be to see me in possession of the husband
you vainly strove to win! Poor woman! I can
make allowance for you. But there must be no
tampering with my husband now. He is entirely
mine; and you shall have no opportunity of practising your wiles and blandishments upon him.
I'll look to that." And, accordingly, in the
chance intercourse which took place between the
parties, Mrs. Mahon was never very far from her
husband's side, and would remain a silent and
attentive listener to any conversation that might
be going on between Lady De Marbury and her
clergyman. Indeed, she has been known rudely
to interrupt the conversation, and summon her
husband to her side, if he seemed too attentive to
her ladyship, or to manifest any desire again to
cultivate her acquaintance.

It is probable that poor Mac had no very easy
time of it with his wife. She was said to be
intensely jealous of him; and, from the necessity

he was under to stand well in the eyes of his flock, especially the female portion of them, he may have given some occasion for those outbursts of jealousy which were very frequent episodes in their matrimonial life.

Mac was not quite such an altered person but that he had some of his countrymen's peculiarities lingering about him. He was naturally partial to the society of the fair sex, and got on with them; he was fond of paying compliments, and could appreciate female beauty when he saw it. Even in the case of Lady De Marbury herself, when he perceived that she meant him no mischief, and that the past was to be buried in oblivion, he would gladly have returned to their former habits of intimacy; but he reckoned without his wife. He soon found the inconvenience of having possessed her of the notion that there had been something of an attachment on the part of Lady De Marbury towards himself in days gone by.

No lioness robbed of her whelps could have displayed greater rage than did Mrs. Mahon at the bare mention of her husband's proposal, that they

should show Lady De Marbury some civility, and
see a little more of her.   Mac got too much of it
the first time he ever broached the subject, to be
willing again to bring on himself such an avalanche
of fury.   It was not pleasant to his feelings to be
called by the wife of his bosom an " Irish adventurer" and an "impostor," and to have the sincerity
of his religious convictions decidedly questioned.
Worse insinuations, if possible, were thrown out;
and there was no knowing where the excited lady
would have stopped, if Mac had not made his
peace by at once promising to give up all intercourse with Lady De Marbury.

This was the first specimen of what his wife
was capable of saying that Mr. Mahon had been
favoured with, and he was in no hurry to provoke
another.   She held the purse, and could very soon
reduce him to submission.

Mrs. Mahon was the widow of a cornchandler
when her husband married her, and she had no
family by either husband.  She was very ordinary-
looking, but dressed in an expensive, showy manner,
and with a great profusion of jewelry; a contrast,

in this respect, to Lady De Marbury, who invariably dressed very plainly and scarcely ever wore ornaments.

Mrs. Mahon's present social position was, of course, considerably elevated above her former one, and, being a woman of a good deal of cleverness, and with much natural quickness, she pushed through her part and contrived to pass muster. She kept her carriage, and gave frequent entertainments, and was altogether popular enough amongst her husband's flock. Young ladies she kept in their place, and had a quick eye for any incipient flirtation with her husband. It was seldom repeated, and Mac would slink away with a sort of half-guilty consciousness from one of these charmers when next they encountered.

As for poor Lady De Marbury, she was constrained to give up visiting at her clergyman's house, so undisguised had Mrs. Mahon's jealousy against her become. I do not know that this exhibition of jealousy was, after all, so very disagreeable to Lady De Marbury, though it was attended with inconvenience, and even annoyance at times.

It seemed a sort of intimation that she was still an
object capable of being viewed as a rival—that she
was not so very *passé*, after all, but that a man might
get attached to her, or that attachment towards her
might revive in his bosom.  It is probable that she
never thought much about it, but that, when anything reminded her of Mrs. Mahon's jealousy, she felt
more kindly disposed towards poor Mac than she
had ever done in her life before ; or was it that
she took a pleasure in tormenting Mrs. Mahon, and
making her feel by what a precarious tenure she
retained her husband's affections?

It is certain that Lady De Marbury attended
the Pentagon as usual, and, whenever she met
Mr. Mahon in some of the poor houses of his district, behaved to him with remarkable cordiality
and friendliness.

No woman ever really dislikes a man for having
been once fond of her, and for having wished to
marry her.  The Fates may have been against
their union.  There may be still insuperable
obstacles in the way of it, as much so as ever.

But Lady De Marbury would have had but very

little of the woman about her if she could have harboured any ill-will against a man whose principal crime consisted in his having made love to her when she was some dozen years younger. Besides, she pitied him, or fancied she pitied him, for being tied to such a virago as his wife. She would have liked to have seen him married to some nice lady-like girl about his own age, and then they might have talked about old times and seen a good deal of each other.

It was surprising, too, how much more naturally and pleasantly poor MacMahon (as we may call him this once) talked when he was off his guard and away from his wife. He was not like the same person. And when he would speak about Donnington, and ask after "John," and have his joke, as of old times, about the crusty old Scotch steward, and praise Mrs. Hulton's beauty and friendliness towards a young Irish parson as he then was, Lady De Marbury felt her heart expand towards him, and wished that she had made more allowance long ago for the youthful indiscretion he had been betrayed into by the natural warmth of the Hibernian temperament, of which he had his full share.

"Lady De Marbury," said he to her one day, as they were walking up and down in front of the Crescent, "I have often wished to say to you how deeply I regret the foolish action I was once guilty of when I lived at Donnington. I have often wondered how I could have committed such an act of absurdity and presumption; but I trust that if you have not forgotten it, yet that, at any rate, you have ceased to remember it against me to my disadvantage."

"This is an opportunity I have long wished for," she said, "to be able to assure you that the regret and compunction is not all on your side, Mr. Mahon. As we get older I suppose we get more forbearing, and allow more for each other's weaknesses. At any rate, I feel now that I acted with unnecessary harshness and precipitation in the instance you refer to. I could not, of course, have entertained your proposal, but I need not have rejected it with the scorn and contumely I

did. We poor, solitary women," added her ladyship pleasantly, "have not so many to care
for us that we can afford to fling back in a
person's face any well-meant and genuine offers of
kindness."

"I will put everything out of my mind, then,
relating to the past in which you are concerned,
save the recollection of your former kindness, and
of the many happy days I have spent at Donnington." This Mr. Mahon said with much feeling.

"And, for my part, I hope you understand me
to say that, if I have ever caused you pain or
uneasiness by any action or word of mine, I now
wish that action undone and that word unsaid.
And if I have ever, even though unintentionally,
led you to suppose that an offer of marriage from
you would not be altogether disagreeable to me,
why, I must blame myself (if any blame there
be about the matter) for the consequences."

With these words they parted; and Mr.
Mahon went to his home not a little moved by a
display of frankness and candour, on Lady De
Marbury's part, of which, indeed, he had not

believed her capable. And it suggested some reflections to his own mind, by way of contrast, for which we may hope he was the better.

He felt almost hourly the inconvenience of having dropped into his wife's narrow mind the idea that Lady De Marbury had once given him encouragement, and he was now reaping the bitter fruits of it.

The ready inference which such a woman as we have described Mrs. Mahon to be would draw from the circumstance would be that there must have been some love-making on her husband's side, as well as on the lady's. "There were six of one and half a dozen of the other: probably the family interfered and put a stop to it;" *so* the irate lady reasoned, and jumped to a conclusion which, though not quite correct, yet had some foundation of truth. And her husband heard enough about it, morning, noon, and night, until he wished most heartily that he had never mentioned Lady De Marbury's name to her, or that he was back once more in Ireland, in his own native village of Ballydoodle.

Things went on in this way for a considerable time, Mr. Mahon doing all he could, for the sake of his position in the town, to conceal these domestic bickerings from the knowledge of his flock. Poor man ! he forgot that servants have ears, and tongues too, which they are never slow to make use of when there is any domestic scandal stirring.

It oozed out, then, that matters were not going on very comfortably between the minister of the Pentagon and his rich wife. Scenes between them were even described—with additions, probably. For it was hardly conceivable that a woman would hurl a china tea-pot at her husband's head, and one, too, that had cost so much money. However, it was said that she did so, and that the cause was jealousy.

Rumours now were rife enough in Bath. There was to be a separation, it was said. He treated his wife badly : she had discovered that he had a wife in Ireland.

These and such-like rumours were buzzed about from one to another, and there was some fresh scandal every day.

U

Poor Mahon's chapel was more crowded than ever; though it was a doubtful symptom of the state of the popular mind, at best. People were anxious to see how he looked, to hear if he would make any allusion to the reports that were in circulation about him. He had all the ladies on his side (they always do side against the wife). The fathers and brothers only were sceptical, and had their "own opinion" about the business— that Mahon was "no better than he ought to be. There was probably something in that story about another wife in Ireland: such things, it is well known, are thought nothing of there."

Lady De Marbury occupied her place as usual Sunday after Sunday. Her name had not been openly talked of. People did not like to let their tongues loose about the daughter of Lord Clapham.

Mrs. Mahon herself even used some reticence about naming (except to her husband) one who stood so high in the religious world, was the person of the greatest rank in her husband's congregation, and was so indefatigable in going about amongst the poor and relieving them.

But, if she spared Lady De Marbury's name, it was more than she did with regard to Miss This and Miss The Other, whom she was perpetually casting up in her husband's teeth, and with whom she almost carried on open warfare when they encountered in public.

This was a pleasing source of excitement to the young ladies in question. They rather liked it, and it made them of importance in the place. They were quite a match for Mrs. Mahon any day, and defied her wrath. They would talk to Mr. Mahon as much as they pleased, and his wife might do her worst. At length it was generally known that Mrs. Mahon had gone to Cheltenham for "her health," and that her husband was now alone in the field.

This was the signal for an inundation of worked slippers, anti-macassars (they were then in fashion), ottoman-covers, foot-stools—anything that female ingenuity could devise. Nor were there wanting more substantial "tokens of respect," wrung out of only half-convinced fathers, and entirely scep- tical brothers, in the shape of a handsome service

of plate, with a purse containing a couple of
hundred sovereigns.

Nor was Lady De Marbury's supplemental present of a few dozen of wine the least acceptable of
the many testimonials of liking and sympathy
which poured in upon Mr. Mahon, now deprived
of the company of his wife.

It must be admitted that Mac did not take much
to heart the loss of her society. So things went
on for some time, Mr. Mahon still retaining his
hold over the minds of the congregation that
assembled for worship at the Pentagon. His wife
never troubled him, and was contented to remain
at Cheltenham until her husband showed signs
of contrition, which, it must be admitted, were
very slow in coming.

She continued, however, to pay the rent and
taxes of the very handsome house he occupied in
Bath, and, as long as she did this (which, having
taken the house herself, and for a term, she could
not very well avoid doing), her husband was quite
willing that she should prolong her absence to any
extent she pleased.

But though prosperity seemed to attend Mr. Mahon for some time, it was not destined to be very long-lived. Fortune appeared to be tired of befriending him. Breakers ahead made their appearance.

The danger proceeded, in this instance, from an unexpected quarter. An uncouth-looking curate had been lately turned adrift from the Abbey Church, where he had offended the aristocratical members of the congregation by a species of low buffoonery in the pulpit, and by his habit of saying whatever came uppermost in his mind while preaching—however ridiculous, or even irreverent, the sentiment might happen to be.

Mr. Bunning had been formerly a Dissenting preacher, and had got ordained through one of those back doors into the Church's ministry which exist in this country in the shape of cheap theological colleges. He was very voluble, had a good deal of humour and drollery about him, and a certain degree of smartness and cleverness.

It was impossible to refrain from smiling at some of the ludicrous things he would introduce into his sermons without apparently being in the least conscious of the indecorum he was guilty of. He has been known, in the pulpit, and amidst the scarcely-repressed titters of his hearers, to quote the lines—

> " When the devil was sick,
> The devil a monk would be :
> When the devil was well,
> The devil a monk was he."

And he had a choice collection of similar sayings, which he would produce on the most inappropriate occasions.

Well, will it be believed that such a man had his admirers ? He was supposed, in his own coarse way, often to hit the right nail on the head. He kept up people's attention, it was said—he certainly did that. Many who would pay no attention to ordinary exhortations would be struck with the pithiness of some of Mr. Bunning's sayings, and could not well help remembering and (it might happen) acting upon them.

This was what his admirers said in his behalf. And no sooner had he been ejected from his curacy—with very little ceremony, too—than a proprietary chapel, called the Heptagon, was at once engaged and licensed for him, and there he forthwith commenced his ministrations.

The Heptagon was situated at a very short distance from Mr. Mahon's chapel, and the popularity of the new preacher at once told upon the congregation of the latter place: many who went to hear and to be amused at first, ended in taking sittings.

There was more *in* Mr. Bunning's sermons, it was said, than there was in Mr. Mahon's; and it must be admitted that poor Mac's *were* rather diffuse and overlaid with imagery. However poetical and beautiful as compositions, yet they were thoroughly *useless* sermons, without any definite aim or object; while Mr. Bunning's (whatever else they were) were pointed and telling enough, and it would certainly have been no easy matter to have gone to sleep under his ministry.

Poor Mahon's congregation fell off by degrees. People were getting tired of him; and it may be that there was some truth in what was whispered about him—that he was getting lazy, and was rather too fond of dining out. He was not at all the favourite he had been, that was certain.

Lady De Marbury watched these symptoms of declining popularity with concern. She had a sort of kindness for Mr. Mahon, from old associations; and though his ministrations were not exactly to her mind—never had been, in fact— yet she was unwilling to desert him in his need. So she continued to attend the Pentagon with the same regularity as before, even though the numerous empty pews presented such a depressing sight, especially to one of her ladyship's school, who delight in crowded churches and to " sit under " an " acceptable minister."

Luckily, at this time old Lord Portbury, who was at the head of the Indian Board, happened to come to Bath to drink the waters. He was brother-in-law to the late Lord Clapham, they having married sisters, and was consequently uncle, by marriage, to Lady De Marbury.

To him she at once applied herself, and, by dint

of a little perseverance, obtained for Mr. Mahon (whom the noble viscount was induced to go and hear) an appointment to an Indian chaplaincy.

He was only too glad to exchange for it his incumbency of the Pentagon, which was becoming more and more unprofitable, in every sense of the word.

He shortly afterwards sailed for India, and I have never heard of his death, nor can I say whether he has been joined by his wife : she certainly did not go out with him.

There was nothing very much to admire in poor Mac's character, it must be allowed, and not a little to condemn ; but, on the whole, we must be glad that he found such a friend as he did in Lady De Marbury.

## CHAPTER XXII.

IT frequently happens that a man is the possessor of an amount of ability and energy for which he has never got the credit from others, and which, to a great extent, has been unknown to himself. Opportunity or necessity has been the means of developing his hidden resources, and he astonishes the world and himself by the rapidity with which he seizes on a foremost place amongst writers, or speakers, or workers.

Sir John De Marbury was an illustration of this. He had passed, in the estimation of his neighbours, as a man of pleasure, as a man vain of his position, as setting a great store upon the advantages which that position gave him. He was known, indeed, to be far from wanting in intelligence, and that he could readily make himself master of any subject he applied himself to. He was not much of a reader of books, indeed, but he was of the great page of human nature; and it might be said of him that nothing escaped his notice, or was lost on him, which fell within his range of observation.

His travels abroad, too, which, owing to his peculiar circumstances, were unusually prolonged, had not been of that aimless and desultory character which rambles on the Continent usually are, and they had undoubtedly tended to enlarge his mind and mature many a half-developed conception. At Geneva, in particular, he had cultivated the literary society of the place, and seemed to have imbibed some of that spirit of freedom of inquiry which appears to be indigenous to it.

When he returned to Cheshire with his wife, and began to take part again in county business, it was soon seen that a change had come over him. He had married a wife with no pretensions to aristocratical birth. She was one of the people— one of that large family of workers by whose

incessant toil he, and such as he, were enabled
to take their ease. From henceforth he would
identify himself with *their* interests, and endeavour
to elevate them to the rank they were entitled to
hold—that of a free, enlightened, and *educated*
English peasantry.

These were his sentiments, and he was not
backward in proclaiming them. He called himself a Tory, but it must have been of a class for
which we have to turn back the page of history
for a good century and a half.

The Tories, he was in the habit of saying, were
the natural friends and allies of the people; and he
expressed but little sympathy with the narrow and
exclusive views which he found dominant upon
his return to his native county.

This was the time when "young England" was
so much talked about. No one exactly knew what
was meant by the term, or what principles the
party professed; and I believe that, down to the
present time, we are not much enlightened upon
the subject. It seemed to be a sort of High
Church Chartism.

The priests and nobles of the land were to put themselves at the head of the peasantry; but who were to be demolished remained a mystery— probably the Whigs.

Their only foreign policy seemed to consist in the restoration of Don Carlos to the Spanish throne, and their home views to be identified with such things as free and unappropriated churches, more frequent holidays for the people, rustic sports on Sundays, curbing the spirit of commercial enterprise throughout the country, and substituting for it the predominance of the landed interests.

Such views, vague and mystified, and incapable of being carried out into practice, as they were, had yet their attraction for a character such as Sir John De Marbury's.

To a generous mind there is always something noble in stripping one's self of the adventitious trappings of wealth and station, and descending to take your place amongst the workers in this busy world, and to win, by your own exertions, what, without worth or deserving on your part, would have been readily accorded to your rank and position in society.

A life of ease and indolence at Donnington seemed to be an ignoble thing, after all; and county business and magistrates' meetings lay no great burden, when all is said and done, upon the intellectual powers.

Sir John needed a wider sphere for his exertions. He would go into Parliament if the chance came in his way. He was now, by the death of his uncle, Lord Clapham (who died of decline at Rome), a rich man, having succeeded, by the terms of his grandfather's will, to large landed estates in Lancashire. He could afford a contest, therefore.

The county was not to be thought of. That was sacred ground; and he would have lost caste for ever if it was known that he had any hankering after what was looked upon as the inalienable patrimony of two or three powerful county families. The son succeeded the father, as a matter of course, if there was a son in the case, and if he wished to sit in Parliament. Otherwise, a relation (the nearer the better) would be sought out, who had a standing of his own in the county as well, and in due time he would be declared a representative of the people.

Newchurch was something of a close borough itself. It was a very aristocratic little town, and most of the tradespeople were dependent for their custom upon the gentry of the town and neighbourhood. It had always returned two members to Parliament.

At the period of the passing of the Reform Bill a great effort had been made to disfranchise this borough, or at any rate to strike off one of its members. But local interest had proved too strong.

By a kind of understanding between the heads of the borough and some of the influential families in the neighbourhood, a Conservative and a Liberal had been always returned. There had never been any opposition, or whisper of it. The two present members had held their seats for years. They were closely related to each other, and, though avowedly of different politics, were marvellously alike in their conduct, their differences being principally confined to the hustings.

When the farce of electing them as representatives of the people had been gone through, little more was heard of them until the period of the next general election. Their names, indeed, would figure in the division-lists; that was all. Each stood by his party, and could be reckoned upon when any great struggle between the "ins and the outs" was to come off. But the main interest of these two worthy gentlemen's lives was centred in the clubs and other haunts of fashion. To be in Parliament afforded them just occupation enough to prevent them dying of *ennui*. They were both eldest sons, and their fathers were great landed proprietors in the county. One of them was Lord Powderham's eldest son, the Honourable Grenville North, and the other was his first cousin, Mr. North Grenville. They had always been in the habit of taking matters very quietly, and could hardly credit the intelligence that reached them, that there was some idea of contesting one or both of the seats at the ensuing general election.

Newchurch, people said, was a borough of importance, and had a considerable silk trade of its own. It was desirable that one of its members, at least, should be competent to look after its interests, and pay attention to local representations.

Sir John De Marbury was solicited to stand, but for some time he declined, as being unwilling to oppose either of the existing members, with whom he was on terms of intimacy. At length the difficulty was got over by the retirement of one of them—Mr. North—principally on account of his father's advanced age, which made his own elevation to the Upper House a thing of probable occurrence before any great length of time should elapse. There was a talk, indeed, of substituting for him a younger brother; but, as Sir John was promptly in the field as soon as ever Mr. North's intention not to offer himself again was known for certain, the design was abandoned. Here was a wide field of usefulness and of ambition now open to Sir John De Marbury; and *how* amply he availed himself of it the records of Parliament sufficiently show, though it does not fall within our present purpose to enter upon the subject.

There was no opposition to his election. His views, though, perhaps, Utopian upon some points, were those of a high-minded English gentleman, bent upon doing his duty, and elevating the moral and social condition of those in a humbler condition of life than himself. And it was a proud day for Donnington, and for *her* who sat in her open carriage near the hustings, her little brothers by her side, and who listened with glistening eyes to the manly, generous sentiments that proceeded from her husband's lips, when the Mayor declared North Grenville, of Norton Booths Park, Esquire, and Sir John De Marbury, of Donnington Hall, Baronet, to be duly elected as members to serve in Parliament for the borough of Newchurch.

———

Sir John De Marbury still lives, though he is no longer designated by the title which he in-

herited from his father; and she whom we have
known as Annie Delves lends grace and dignity
to that shining band of gold which now encircles
her brow.

THE END.

WILLIAM STEVENS, PRINTER, 37, BELL YARD, TEMPLE BAR.

# ST. KNIGHTON'S KEIVE:

## A CORNISH TALE.

"Abounds in masterly descriptions of the wild and beautiful scenery of that desolate land."—*John Bull.*

"A most interesting volume. . . . The various incidents are well told, the scenery of this grandly wild country is admirably described, and the manners, religious tendencies, &c., of the Cornish miners are vividly and truthfully portrayed. . . . The majority of novels in the present day are so worthless, that it is gratifying to meet with a well-written, entertaining, and instructive story. 'St. Knighton's Keive' will aid in passing some hours away most pleasantly."—*The Press.*

"Affords some curious glimpses of Cornish manners and customs."—*Weekly Dispatch.*

"This book . . . . we would recommend to summer tourists. Sea-side libraries will welcome it."—*Reader.*

SMITH, ELDER, & CO., 65, CORNHILL.